Mary Anne + 2 Many Babies

**Other books by
Ann M. Martin**

Rachel Parker, Kindergarten Show-off

Eleven Kids, One Summer

Ma and Pa Dracula

Yours Turly, Shirley

Ten Kids, No Pets

Slam Book

Just a Summer Romance

Missing Since Monday

With You and Without You

Me and Katie (the Pest)

Stage Fright

Inside Out

Bummer Summer

BABY-SITTERS LITTLE SISTER series
THE BABY-SITTERS CLUB mysteries
THE BABY-SITTERS CLUB series

Mary Anne + 2 Many Babies

Ann M. Martin

AN
APPLE
PAPERBACK

SCHOLASTIC INC.
New York Toronto London Auckland Sydney

Cover art by Hodges Soileau

ISBN 0-590-92577-6

12 11 10 9 8 7 6 5 4 3   9   8 9/9 0 1/0

Printed in the U.S.A.   40

This book is for Alice,
my friend from around the world

CHAPTER 1

I was thirteen years old before I became a sister, and guess what. My new sister was my age, thirteen. Were we long-lost twins, separated at birth and reunited thirteen years later? No. Although that's much more interesting than the truth. The truth is that my sister is actually my stepsister. Earlier this year, my father got married again, and he happened to marry the mother of Dawn Schafer, who was already one of my best friends. So Dawn and I changed from best friends to best friends *and* sisters. Not many kids are that lucky.

My name is Mary Anne Spier. I'm an eighth-grader at Stoneybrook Middle School (commonly known as SMS) in Stoneybrook, Connecticut. I was born here and have lived here all my life. Before Dawn came along, I had a very small family. Two people. My dad and me. Of course, I had a mom in the beginning, but she died when I was really small. I don't even remember her. After she died, Dad raised me. He did a good job, even if he was strict, but I always wished for a bigger family; at the very least for a baby brother or sister.

When I was twelve and in seventh grade, a new family moved to Stoneybrook — Dawn and Jeff Schafer and their mother. The Schafers had just been divorced, and Mrs. Schafer wanted to raise her kids in the town in which she'd grown up. That town was Stoneybrook. Unfortunately for Dawn and Jeff, *they* had grown up in California, so the move to cold, snowy Connecticut was something of a shock to them. Dawn was determined to make the best of things, though, and she adjusted to her new life fairly quickly. For one thing, she made new friends right away. I was her first friend, and I introduced her to my friends in the Baby-sitters Club, which is a business we run. (I'll explain that later.) Right away, Dawn and I started spending a lot of time at one another's houses, and guess what we discovered one day when we were looking through our parents' high school yearbooks. We found out that a long time ago my dad had dated her mom. They'd been sweethearts. But then they graduated from high school, and Dawn's mother went off to college in California and met Mr. Schafer and married him and eventually had Dawn and Jeff. Meanwhile, my dad had also gotten married, although he'd remained in Stoneybrook.

Well, Dawn and I knew just what to do with our secret. We arranged for our parents to meet again, and after awhile they began dating, then *finally* they got married. (In case you're wondering, Jeff moved back to California to live with his father. That happened before his mom married my dad. He was simply never happy in Connecticut. He missed his old life too much. I love Jeff, but I hardly ever see him.)

"Dawn? How come the hedge clippers are in the bread drawer?" I asked one day. It was a Monday afternoon. School was over, and Dawn and I were prowling around the kitchen, fixing a snack.

Dawn shrugged. "Mom's responsible, I'm sure. I'll put them back."

Dawn took the clippers from me and headed for the door to the garage. She was smiling.

Dawn's mother, whom she calls Mom and I call Sharon, is just a teensy bit, oh, scatterbrained. Sharon is really nice, and I'm lucky she's my stepmother, but I'm just not *used* to finding hedge clippers in the bread drawer, or my sweater in the freezer, or the TV remote control on a shelf in the bathroom. I grew up with a father who could have run for the presidency of the Neat People's Society. Dawn grew up with a mother who wouldn't have been allowed within miles of a meeting of the NPS. Actually, she isn't so much messy as she is completely disorganized — as opposed to my father, who color-codes his socks. How they became friends is beyond me. How they became husband and wife is, I think, beyond even *them*, but they do love each other. And the four of us are learning how to live together without going batty. A few months ago, I might have freaked out if I found a pair of hedge clippers in the bread drawer. Now I can handle the situation calmly.

Dawn returned from the garage, and we sat at the kitchen table with snacks in front of us. Mine was a nice, normal after-school snack — an apple and a handful of chocolate chip cookies. Dawn's was a salad bar — a carrot stick, a zucchini stick, a celery stick, a radish, a little square of tofu, and a small container of uncooked peas. This is an example of a difference between Dawn and me, and between her mom and my dad. Dad and I eat the kind of food we were brought up on, a little of everything — fruits, vegetables, dairy stuff, meat, sweets. Dawn and her mom think it's practically a felony to eat meat. Or sugar. A really great dessert for Dawn is, like, some berries. Now, I am not, I repeat *not*, addicted to junk food the way our friend Claudia Kishi is, but excuse me, berries are not dessert as far as I'm concerned. Cake is dessert. Chocolate pie is dessert. A large brownie is dessert. *Maybe* berries are dessert, but only if a piece of cheesecake is underneath them.

Dawn poked around at her peas, and I bit into my apple.

"I saw the twins' baby brother this morning," said Dawn. (We have friends — not close friends, just school friends — who are twins. Their names are Mariah and Miranda Shillaber, and they have a brother who is just a year and a half old.)

"You did?" I said. "Where? Is he adorable?"

"Yeah, he's pretty cute. He was with Mrs. Shillaber. They'd dropped off Mariah and Miranda at school."

"The twins are so lucky," I said. "I wish our parents would have a baby. They still could, you know. It isn't too late."

"And if my mom doesn't want to give *birth* to another baby," added Dawn, "then she and Richard could adopt one." (Richard is my father.)

"I know. It worked for Kristy's family."

The parents of one of our close friends, Kristy Thomas (who's also a member of the Baby-sitters Club), adopted a two-and-a-half-year-old Vietnamese girl. And they already had six kids between them.

"My mother wouldn't even have to quit work," said Dawn. "Kristy's mother still works. Of course, her grandmother lives there now."

"Yeah. I'm not sure we could convince a grandparent to pick up and move in with us. A baby *is* sort of a big job."

"I guess. But who could take better care of a baby than *us*? We're expert sitters, after all. I mean, we do belong to the Baby-sitters Club."

"By the way, what time is it?" I asked.

"Four-thirty. Our meeting won't start for an hour."

"Okay. I just don't want to be late. You know Kristy."

Dawn rolled her eyes. She knew all right.

We went back to our snacks. After a few moments, Dawn said, "Do you *believe* that new course we have to take? Instead of career class?"

"What? Modern Living?" I replied.

"Yes! I've never heard of such a thing. We're going to learn about marriage? And job hunting? And family finances? And *divorce*? I think I already know enough about divorce, thank you."

"I guess it is sort of weird. At least Logan will be in my class." Not to brag or anything, but Logan Bruno is my boyfriend. We've been

6

going out together for a pretty long time — even though we have definitely had our ups and downs. I'm the only member of the Baby-sitters Club to have a *steady* boyfriend. If you knew Logan you'd understand why I like him. He's kind and caring and funny. He's really gentle, but he also plays great baseball and football. Plus, he's cute.

"My homeroom teacher," Dawn spoke up, "said we have to take Modern Living because — and this is a direct quote — 'it's important that we explore and experience the realities of being an adult in today's changing society.' "

"That sounds like an introduction to a really bad social studies filmstrip," I said.

Dawn giggled. "I don't think it's fair that only the eighth-graders are subjected to this torture. Don't the sixth- and seventh-graders need to know how to be adults, too?"

"Yes," I answered, "but they'll get their turns when they reach eighth grade."

I finished the last of my cookies, swept the crumbs off the table, and stood up. Dawn cleared away our napkins. (Her mother may be messy, but Dawn is neat and organized.)

"We better go," said Dawn.

"Okay. Oh, I have to feed Tigger first!" Tigger is my gray tiger-striped kitten. When Dad and I moved out of our house and into the old farmhouse Dawn's mom had bought, Tigger came with us. He's our only pet. I love him to bits. (I think Sharon is still getting used to him. I don't know what's taking her so long. He's absolutely adorable.)

I scooped up some kibble into Tigger's dish. Dawn looked at her watch again. "Now we *really* better go," she said.

"Okay. I'm ready." My sister and I left for Claudia Kishi's house.

CHAPTER 2

I still feel a little funny riding my bike to Claud's. That's because I used to live across the street from her. Riding my bike from one side of the street to the other would have been sort of silly. But my new house isn't nearby. I can still run inside the Kishis' house without bothering to ring the bell, though. Kristy and I did that when we were little. (Kristy also used to live across from Claud, next door to me, but she's moved, too.) And we continue to do it. So do the rest of the members of the Baby-sitters Club (or BSC).

Dawn and I dashed upstairs and hightailed it past the door of Claud's older sister, Janine the Genius. She wasn't there, though. Then we ran into Claudia's room, picked our way over the junk on her floor, and flopped onto her bed. I was pleased to see that we were not the last club members to arrive.

"Hi, guys," Dawn greeted Claudia, Kristy, and Jessi Ramsey.

"Hi," they replied. (If we didn't sound overly enthusiastic, remember that we'd seen each other in school just a couple of hours earlier.)

Kristy Thomas was sitting in Claudia's director's chair, her visor perched on her head, a pencil stuck over one ear.

Kristy is the president. (Of BSC, I mean.)

Jessi, one of our junior officers, was leafing through the club notebook.

As I found a comfortable position on the bed, I glanced at Kristy. She was staring at Claud's digital clock. That clock is the official club timepiece, and when the numbers flip from 5:29 to 5:30, Kristy begins a meeting, whether all the club members are present or not.

I guess Kristy has a right to do that. After all, she's not just the club president, she's the person who started the BSC. The club was her idea. What is the BSC? It's really a business, and a successful one. This is how it works. Three times a week — on Mondays, Wednesdays, and Fridays, from five-thirty until six — my friends and I gather in Claud's room and wait for parents to call us, needing baby-sitters. When a call comes in, one of us agrees to take on the job. This is great for parents.

They make one phone call and reach seven people, seven expert baby-sitters. So they're bound to line up a sitter quickly. They don't have to call one person after another, trying to find someone available.

How do parents know when to call us? How do they know when we hold our meetings? Because we advertise — you know, flyers and posters. Also because we've been in business for awhile now. We have a good reputation.

Anyway, Kristy is the president, since she started the BSC. She is overflowing with fantastic ideas. Kristy is the one who thought of keeping a club notebook, which is like a diary. Each time one of us finishes a sitting job, we're supposed to write about it in the book. Then, once a week, we read through the recent entries to find out what happened on our friends' jobs. This has turned out to be really helpful.

Kristy also came up with the idea for Kid-Kits. Every member of the club has made a Kid-Kit. A Kid-Kit is a large box that has been painted, decorated, and filled with child-appealing items — our old games, books, and toys, art supplies, activity books, and so forth. Our sitting charges just love to see us show up with our Kid-Kits. They may have the most spectacular toys ever created, but show them something new (even if it's old, it's new to the kids), and suddenly it's more interesting than anything they own. Somehow Kristy knew that.

Kristy seems to be a natural with kids. She's certainly around them enough at her own house, although for the longest time only one of her brothers and sisters was younger than she was. Hmm — that's pretty confusing. What I mean is, Kristy's mom got remarried just like my dad, and when that happened, her family changed. A lot. When Kristy and I used to live next door to each other, her family consisted of her two older brothers, Sam and Charlie; her little brother, David Michael; and her mom. Her dad had walked out when David Michael was just a baby. Several years later, her mom began dating this guy Watson Brewer, who happens to be a millionaire. He also happens to be divorced, the father of two little kids. After Mrs. Thomas and Watson Brewer got married, the Thomases moved across town into Watson's mansion. That was when Kristy's family began to grow. The Brewers adopted Emily Michelle, the little girl from Vietnam. Nannie, Kristy's grandmother, moved in to help care for her. Plus, Watson's children, Karen and Andrew, live at their father's every other weekend. Also, they acquired a dog and two goldfish, and Watson already owned a cat.

Did I tell you that Kristy is my other best

friend? Actually, she's my first best friend, since we grew up together, and I didn't meet Dawn until the middle of seventh grade. A lot of people think Kristy and I make a pretty weird duo. That's because we're so different. Kristy is extremely outgoing and is known for her big mouth. (Well, she is.) Plus, she loves sports and even coaches a softball team for little kids. (Her team is called Kristy's Krushers!) I, on the other hand, am shy. I'm whatever you call the opposite of outgoing. (Ingoing? Ingrown?) I think before I speak. I'm romantic (maybe that's why I ended up with a steady boyfriend before any of the other BSC members did), I cry easily (nobody likes to go to the movies with me), and I do *not* enjoy sports. However, Kristy and I look sort of alike. Everyone says so. Our faces are shaped the same way, we both have brown hair and brown eyes, and we're short for thirteen. We dress differently, though. Kristy's happiest when she can just drag on a pair of jeans, a turtleneck shirt, a sweat shirt, her running shoes, and maybe a baseball cap. (Her uniform.) She never bothers with jewelry or makeup. (Well, hardly ever.) I wear clothes that are a little more trendy — as trendy as my dad will allow me to look. Mostly, I guess I'm on the preppy side. I don't have pierced ears (neither does Kristy), but I do wear jewelry, including clip-on earrings. And I experiment with my hair sometimes. No major dos, though. So Kristy and I are quite different. Maybe that's why we've been such good friends. We complement each other, personality-wise.

You know who's the opposite of us in almost every way? Claudia. Yet she's a good friend, too. We voted Claud the vice-president of the BSC. We thought that was fair, considering we meet in her room three times a week, mess it up (usually), take over her phone, and eat her junk food. The phone — that's another reason we hold our meetings in her room. Claud has not only her own extension, but her very own phone number. That means that when job calls come in, we don't tie up someone else's line, just Claud's. You may think Claudia's job isn't difficult. I know it sounds that way, until you realize that not everyone remembers to call the BSC during our meetings. When parents call during off-hours, Claud has to deal with those jobs.

In what ways is Claud different from Kristy and me? All right, let me see. First, she comes from a smaller, less complicated family. It consists of her parents and Janine. No pets. And Claud's interests are art, junk food, mysteries, baby-sitting, and fashion, although probably not in that order. Claudia is a fantastic artist,

14

and she's addicted to junk food and Nancy Drew mysteries. Candy, chips, and books are hidden all over her room. (They're hidden because her parents disapprove of both addictions. They wish she would eat healthy foods and read the classics.)

Claud is also very fashion conscious, unlike Kristy and me. To begin with, she's exotic-looking. No brown hair and brown eyes for her. Claud is Japanese-American. Her hair is jet black, long, and silky. Her dark eyes are almond-shaped. Her skin is creamy and clear (despite the junk food she consumes). She loves to experiment with her hair, braiding it, twisting it up, wearing ribbons and barrettes and ornaments in it. And her clothes are outrageous. Her parents let her dress in whatever style she likes. A typical Claudia outfit might include a sequined shirt, stirrup pants (maybe black), low black boots, dangly turquoise earrings, and ribbons woven through tiny braids in her hair. And she wouldn't forget sparkly nail polish.

Another thing about Claud. She's a *terrible* student. She could be a good one if she tried, but school doesn't interest her. Sometimes her awful spelling drives me crazy — but I love her anyway.

"Hi, everyone!"

"Hey, Stace!" we replied.

Stacey McGill had dashed into club head-quarters, followed closely by Mallory Pike. They had arrived *just* in time. As soon as they sat down (Mal on the floor with Jessi; Stacey backward in the desk chair), Kristy announced, "This meeting of the Baby-sitters Club will now come to order. Any important business?"

"Dues day!" cried Stacey. She's the treasurer, and one of her jobs is to collect dues from the seven main club members every Monday. (Two more people belong to the club, but they do not attend meetings and don't have to pay dues. They're associate members, kids we can call on to baby-sit if a BSC call comes in and none of us can take the job. Guess what. One of the associate members is . . . Logan!) Anyway, Stace is great at math, so she's the perfect choice for keeping track of the money in our treasury, which is a manila envelope. We use the money to cover our expenses: to help Claudia pay her phone bill, to buy new items to replace used-up ones in the Kid-Kits, and so forth.

Like Claud, Stacey is a real fashion plate. She dresses wildly, wears lots of jewelry (her ears are pierced; so are Claudia's), and her mom lets her get her blonde hair permed. Stacey grew up in New York City. In fact, like

Dawn, she didn't move to Stoneybrook until seventh grade. Recently, her parents got divorced, which has been tough on Stace. Now she lives with her mom, while her dad is back in NYC. Stacey has no brothers or sisters. Also no pets. She's funny, outgoing, caring, wonderful with children, and a teensy bit boy crazy. I really admire Stacey. She's been through a lot, and her troubles seem to make her a stronger person. Apart from the divorce, Stacey has to cope with a medical problem. She has a disease called diabetes. Her body can't break down sugar the way most people's bodies can, so she has to monitor her diet extra carefully (no sweets or desserts), test her blood several times each day, and (this is the gross part) give *herself* injections of insulin. Even so, Stacey winds up in the hospital from time to time, but she always bounces back and is usually pretty cheerful.

What happens if Stacey or one of the other club officers has to miss a meeting? No problem. Dawn takes over for that person. As alternative officer, that's her job. She has to know everything about running the club, but that's easy for Dawn Schafer, since she's almost as organized and neat as my father is.

Dawn is also very much an individual,

which is one of the reasons she became the second of my two best friends. I like her independence, even though I eventually learned that individuality plus independence does not necessarily equal self-confidence. Dawn has some chinks in her armor just like everyone else. In general, though, she's easygoing and not likely to be swayed by what other people are doing or thinking.

Dawn has the most amazing hair I have ever seen. It's at least as long as Claud's, just as silky, but as light as Claud's is dark. It's nearly white, sort of the color of sweet corn. Dawn's eyes are blue and sparkly, she's tall and thin, and her clothes are as individual as her personality is. She wears what she feels like wearing and manages to look trendy and casual at the same time. Her mom is not at all strict about what Dawn wears — which may explain why Dawn's ears are double-pierced, so she can wear two pairs of earrings at the same time, although she often wears four non-matching earrings!

Dawn, Kristy, Claudia, Stacey, and I are eighth-graders at SMS. The other two main members are eleven-year-old sixth-graders at SMS. They are Jessi Ramsey and Mallory Pike, our junior officers. "Junior" just means that their parents will allow them to baby-sit only after school or on weekend days; not at night unless they're sitting for their own brothers and sisters. Mal and Jessi are another pair of best friends, and I can see why they are drawn together. Each is the oldest kid in her family: Jessi has a younger sister and a baby brother, and Mal has *seven* younger sisters and brothers. Each loves kids and is a terrific baby-sitter. And each feels that her parents treat her like an infant. They *were* finally allowed to have their ears pierced (only one hole per ear, of course), but Mal, who wears glasses, is not permitted to get contacts, and both have to dress kind of like . . . oh, like me, for instance. On the tame side.

Mal and Jessi adore reading, especially horse stories, but other than that, their interests are pretty different.

Jessi is a ballet dancer, a good one. She takes lessons at a special dance school in Stamford (the city nearest to Stoneybrook). In the mornings, she wakes up early to practice at the *barre* in her basement, and she has performed in lots of big productions. I think she will be a star one day.

Mal, on the other hand, likes to write and draw. She makes up stories and illustrates them. Also, she keeps journals. I bet she will become a children's book author.

In terms of looks, Jessi and Mal are pretty different, too. Jessi's skin is a deep brown, her hair is black, and she has the long legs a dancer needs. Mal is white, her curly hair is red, and she'd give just about anything to get rid of her glasses. Also her braces, even though they're the clear kind and don't show up too much.

Ring, ring!

"I'll get it!" cried Claudia.

Stacey had finished collecting the dues, and now the phone was ringing with what was probably our first job call of the day.

Claud grabbed the receiver. "Hello, Baby-sitters Club." She listened for a moment. "Yes? . . . Oh, hi, Mrs. Salem," she said. (We met Mrs. Salem when we were taking an infant-care class. She and her husband have twin babies, a boy and a girl.) "Sure, sure," Claud was saying. "Okay, I'll call you back in a few minutes. 'Bye." Claudia hung up the phone and turned to me. "That was Mrs. Salem. She needs a sitter for Ricky and Rose next Tuesday afternoon. Who's free?"

I think I forgot to mention that I am the secretary of the BSC. I'm in charge of the club record book. (Guess who thought of keeping a record book.) I write down any important BSC information and I schedule *all* of our jobs.

I looked at the page for the following Tuesday. "Hey, guess what. I'm the only one free," I said. "And I'd *love* to sit for the twins. Babies. I can't wait!"

Claud phoned Mrs. Salem to give her the good news.

CHAPTER 3

"Do you, Mary Anne Spier. take this man to be your husband?"

"I do."

"And do you, Logan Bruno, take this woman to be your wife?"

"I do."

"I now pronounce you husband and wife, for as long as you are members of my Modern Living class."

I had never been so embarrassed. It was the second session of Modern Living, and everyone in our class had to pair up and get married. At least Mrs. Boyden hadn't asked Logan to kiss me.

Why were we getting married? Good question. I'll give you Mrs. Boyden's answer. "Class," she had said during our first session, "you are in eighth grade. Most of you are thirteen years old now. Some of you are four-teen, a few of you are twelve. Despite how old or young you may feel, the truth is that you are now biologically capable of becoming parents, or you will be soon. How many think you are capable of parenting, of being part of a couple, or of living on your own?"

I didn't know about living on my own or getting married, but I certainly knew every-thing about taking care of kids.

So I raised my hand.

I didn't realize Mrs. Boyden would call on me. I'd thought she was just asking for a show of hands. But she said, "Mary Anne?"

"Yes?" I replied. "Oh. Um, well, I baby-sit all the time," I said, my face flushing. "I can change diapers and everything."

Mrs. Boyden had not seemed too impressed. She had just nodded. And then she had started talking about getting married. "The best way to experience adult life is to live it," she said. "That's why you are going to pair up, get married, and stay married until this class is over. You may choose your partners if you wish. I will assign partners to those students who do not choose their own."

Nearby, someone whispered, "Like getting married to someone you see three times a week is realistic."

I had glanced at Logan then, who was sitting on my other side. He'd smiled at me. We were going to "get married." It was an exciting prospect. *I* knew we were ready to take the big step. Well, I thought we were. Okay, I wasn't sure at all, but I definitely wanted to find out. Especially if it meant we could spend more time together.

Our class had spent the rest of that first session talking about stuff like how old our parents were when they got married, and what being married *really* means. I had dared to raise my hand to contribute to the conversation, but only after Shawna Riverson had said, "I think getting married *really* means that you have, like, a plastic bride and groom on your wedding cake, not those little bride and groom mice or something. Or maybe you could have, like, a giant plastic wedding bell and some bluebirds or something."

The class snickered, and even Mrs. Boyden looked surprised.

Well, after a comment like that, nothing I said could sound any more stupid. So I raised my hand. "I think marriage really means commitment. It means you love your husband or wife so much that when you have a problem, you try to work it out so you can stay together."

"You are definitely on the right track," Mrs. Boyden said to me. "Thank you, Mary Anne. Class, there's a little more to marriage than the wedding. That's just the first *day*."

Even so, we had our shot at weddings in the very next session of Modern Living. "Are all of you engaged to be married?" asked Mrs. Boyden at the beginning of class.

Four boys raised their hands. *"We* aren't," they said, looking disgusted. And Gordon Brown added, "There are nine girls and thirteen boys in this class, Mrs. Boyden. All the girls have been taken."

"We have not been 'taken'!" cried Erica Blumberg. "We are not pieces of property. You can't claim us."

"Sheesh," said Gordon. "All right, the girls have all been used up."

Erica's face practically turned purple. "We are not hot water, either. We aren't some commodity. You can't use us up."

"Commodity?" I heard Shawna whisper. "Doesn't she mean condiment?" Shawna looked really pleased with herself.

"Okay, okay, kids. Please calm down," said Mrs. Boyden, holding her hands in the air. "We'll discuss this some other time. Gordon, you're right. Two of our couples will consist of boys only. How do you want to handle that?"

"I am *not* going to be a girl," said Howie Johnson.

"Well, neither am I," said Gordon and the other boys.

"Do they have to decide ahead of time who's the wife and who's the husband?" asked Logan. "Maybe they could decide later. Maybe they wouldn't even have to tell us their decisions."

Mrs. Boyden opened her mouth to say something, but before she could start speaking, Howie said, "Yeah, yeah. We'll decide later."

"Okay," replied our teacher, in that tone of voice grown-ups use when they *mean*, "If that's the way you want it, but I think it's a pretty poor idea. I guess you'll just have to find out for yourselves."

The girls and the remaining boys had paired up by themselves. Mrs. Boyden created two couples out of the other four boys because they refused to do it for themselves. Then the marriage ceremonies began, and soon I was Logan Bruno's wife and he was my husband and I was being silently thankful that we didn't have to kiss in front of our entire Modern Living class, not to mention in front of Mrs. Boyden.

"From now on," said our teacher, when the weddings were over, "when you are in class, you will sit together as couples. In fact, when you are in class you will *be* couples, and I'll expect you to think and behave as such. You may be asked to be couples outside of class," she added, and her words sounded somehow ominous. (I glanced at my "husband," and he shrugged his shoulders as if to say, "That doesn't make a difference to us. You and I are already a couple.")

Guess what Mrs. Boyden assigned us for homework. She asked each couple to get together, discuss money and finances, and decide whether they could be a financially independent couple.

"Huh?" said Shawna. "You mean like really rich?"

"No, not independently wealthy," said Mrs. Boyden patiently. "Financially independent. Could you support yourselves? Could you live in your own place and buy groceries and clothes and pay your electricity bill and phone bill and taxes and so forth?"

"Don't all married couples support themselves and pay their bills?" asked Gordon. "Don't all families?"

"No," our teacher replied. "Most do, I suppose, but it doesn't happen by magic. You don't get married and suddenly come into money. So your homework is to figure out how you would fare if tomorrow, say, you were married and on your own." She paused, then she smiled and added, "Actually you *are* married and on your own. How are you going to do?"

Logan and I found out that afternoon. I went to my husband's house as soon as school let out. The house didn't feel like my husband's, though, since my husband's younger brother and sister and mother were also there. Kerry, who's nine, and Hunter, who's five and has terrible allergies, were in the kitchen with us, waiting for Mrs. Bruno to take a bag of popcorn out of the microwave.

"Put it idto two bowls, Bobby," said Hunter stuffily to his mother. "If you do't, thed Kerry hogs it. She eats faster thad be."

"I do not!" exclaimed Kerry.

At that moment, the doorbell rang and so did the phone. Mrs. Bruno reached for the phone, and Kerry ran for the door.

"Dear," Logan said to me, "I apologize for the noise here today. Let's go work in the dining room. We can close the doors."

"All right, sweetheart," I answered, grinning.

Ew!" cried Hunter. "Dear! Sweetheart! You

guys sound like you're barried or subthig."
He sniffed loudly.

"We are," replied Logan. "Hunter, this is
your sister-in-law."

I was eager to get to work. "Come along,
honey," I said to Logan.

We closed ourselves into the dining room.
We were equipped for an afternoon of work —
newspaper, writing pad, pens, calculator,
a bag of cookies, and a Thermos of iced
tea.

"Let's see," I said, when we'd seated ourselves at the table and spread out our things.
"First we'll need a place to live."

"Right." Logan opened the paper to the ads
for apartments for rent. "We'll have to start
small," he said. "We probably won't be able
to afford a house right away. How many bed-
rooms do you want?"

"I think two will be enough at first. One for
us, one for guests."

"Okay . . . two-bedroom apartments. Here's
one. The rent is . . . oh, my lord, it's two
thousand dollars a month!"

"Two *thousand?*" I repeated. "What does the
apartment come with? Fourteen bathrooms
and a private plane?"

"I don't know. Maybe it's in a really fancy
complex. There must be cheaper apartments.

Or maybe two *thousand* was a misprint. Maybe a zero was added by accident."

But it wasn't a misprint. The rent for the cheapest two-bedroom apartment we saw advertised was eight hundred dollars a month.

"We'd have to earn nine thousand, six hundred dollars a year just to pay our *rent*," I said. "How much money do you earn each year, Logan?"

Logan estimated how much money he earned baby-sitting and doing odd jobs. I estimated how much money I earned baby-sitting. We added the figures together. Then we stared at each other with our mouths open.

"We couldn't even pay a month's rent," said Logan.

"Let's look at smaller apartments," I suggested. "We could live in a studio for a few years. That would be okay."

"Only if we found one that rented for, like, thirty cents a month. Remember, we have to buy food and clothes."

"And pay all those bills and taxes and stuff," I added.

Then Logan said, "Just for laughs, let's turn to the ads and see if there are any really big sales at the grocery store."

There were. But we also saw that steak cost a fortune, even on sale. "So we won't eat meat," said Logan. "It's not good for you anyway."

"I don't think we'll eat much of anything," I replied. "Everything is expensive. Even junk food."

"There's just one solution," said Logan.

"What?"

"We'll have to live at home. We are not financially independent."

"Whose home?" I asked.

"Mine. I'm the husband."

"So what? I'm the wife and there's more room at my house."

"But I don't want to live with your dad. He would watch me all the time."

"Well, I don't want to live with my nine-year-old sister-in-law and my five-year-old brother-in-law. Anyway, I want us to have our own place. I want to hang curtains and paint cupboards."

"I don't think they let you do that if you aren't paying rent," said Logan. "We haven't found one of those thirty-cents-a-month places yet."

I sighed. "I know. But there *is* more room at my house."

"Yeah. You're right. Okay. We'll live in your bedroom."

Logan and I wrote up our findings. I knew

Logan would be embarrassed to admit in front of the other guys in our class that he'd be living in a girl's bedroom, but that was our only solution. And no matter how silly we found Modern Living, we wanted to do well in the course.

CHAPTER 4

The Salems' house was quiet.

"Ricky and Rose are asleep," said their mother. She sounded sort of relieved. Also, she looked sort of tired.

"Is anything wrong?" I asked.

"Oh, not really. It's just, you know, *twins*."

That didn't worry me much. Especially considering that the BSC once sat for fourteen children for a week. And that I've baby-sat for Mal's brothers and sisters tons of times and even gone on family vacations with the Pikes, as a mother's helper.

I had arrived at the Salems' house for my afternoon baby-sitting job. School had just ended. I'd gone to my job directly from school. Now I was standing with Mrs. Salem in the kitchen.

"All right," she said. "Let's see. The twins will probably wake up in about half an hour. They'll be hungry then. Their bottles are ready to go. After they've eaten, you can take them for a walk. The stroller's in the garage. They should probably wear sweaters. The emergency phone numbers are here on the refrigerator . . .''

Mrs. Salem is so organized. That's one reason my friends and I like to take care of Ricky and Rose. We haven't had too many opportunities, though. The Salems wouldn't let us baby-sit until the twins reached six months. But now they call us *fairly* regularly.

Mrs. Salem left for her meeting, and I sat at the kitchen table and began my homework. First I looked over my notes from Modern Living class. We were talking about parenting. I didn't see that it was such a big deal; not for a baby-sitter anyway. If everyone would just take a child care course, they'd be prepared.

I was opening my math book when I heard a noise from the second floor. I paused and listened. Definite cooing. I tiptoed upstairs and stopped at the doorway to the bedroom the babies share. Even from out in the hallway, I could smell that baby smell — powder and wipes and lotion and clean clothes and wet washclothes.

I waited for the sound of tears, but instead I heard only the cooing. The babies were talking to each other; at least, that's how it seemed.

"Hi, Rose. Hi, Ricky," I called softly from the hallway. I entered their room quietly. The twins have reached that touchy "fear-of-strangers" phase, and I didn't want to make them cry.

They didn't. The cooing stopped, though. They sat in their cribs, watching me solemnly and silently.

"Hey, Ricky. It's me, Mary Anne. I've taken care of you a few times now." I crossed the yellow carpet to Ricky's white crib. I just adore the way the Salems decorated the twins' nursery. It's bright and airy. Yellow striped curtains hang at the windows. A small shelf is already jammed with picture books. A blue wooden chest, decorated with a painting of Winnie-the-Pooh, holds most of their toys. Under the window stands the changing table. Around the middle of the wall runs a colorful frieze of teddy bears and balloons.

I didn't approach Ricky too closely yet. Instead, I stepped over to Rose's crib and whispered to her.

"Want to be . . . *tickled?*" I finally said.

Rose's face cracked into a smile. A few teeth showed. I tickled her toes gently. When she began to giggle, I lifted her from her crib and laid her on the changing table.

A lot of babies do not like to be changed, for some reason. I can't understand that. Personally, if I were wearing a wet, stinky diaper, I wouldn't even wait for someone else to change it. I'd learn to do it myself.

Rose lay on her back and kicked her feet in the air. She let me remove her diaper, which I dropped in the diaper pail. I know, it sounds old-fashioned. But so what. Mrs. Salem does not put disposable diapers on the babies. She found out how bad they are for the environment, and she switched to cloth diapers, even though she and her husband have to wash *loads* of laundry almost every day. They never complain about this.

I pinned Rose into a fresh diaper. Then I looked around the room. "I guess I better dress you in a fresh outfit," I said. From the twins' closet I took a pale blue dress, smocked across the front. I slipped it onto Rose, then completed her outfit — frilly socks and dainty blue cloth shoes. She looked like a princess.

Ricky's turn. He also let me change him without fussing. Then I dressed him in a red-and-white sailor suit. "You look very handsome," I told him.

I carried the twins (one at a time) to the kitchen. I found that I had to plan ahead with the babies. Managing them took some work. For instance, to move them to the kitchen, I had to place Rose back in her crib, carry Ricky downstairs, fasten him in his high chair, return to the bedroom for Rose, then carry *her* downstairs and fasten *her* into *her* high chair. But so what? The babies were as good as gold.

They even gave themselves their bottles. Mr. and Mrs. Salem must have been pretty happy when the babies learned how to hold onto things.

"Ready for a walk, you guys?" I asked.

Ricky smiled at me, and a drop of milk trickled down his chin.

Rose burped, then grinned.

"Charming," I told her, giggling.

I set the twins in their double stroller and walked them down the Salems' driveway. If I do say so myself, they looked awfully cute, sitting side by side, all dressed up, smiling and cooing. I almost wished they were wearing matching outfits so people would know for sure that they were twins, and not just two unrelated babies.

We set off down the sidewalk. We passed an older woman who paused to smile at Ricky and Rose. Then we met up with a man who stopped to say, "Goodness. Ricky and Rose. You two are certainly getting big. Don't you make a fine-looking pair."

In response, Rose kicked her feet, and Ricky waved his arms around. They gurgled and grinned.

A few minutes later, a couple of little girls

flew through the front door of a house and dashed across their lawn. "Hi, Rosie! Hi, Ricky!" they cried. Then they looked at me. "Lady, can we play with the twins, please?" asked the younger girl.

Lady? Sheesh, was I getting *that* old? I thought. But what I said was, "Sure, for a few minutes. I'm Mary Anne. I'm baby-sitting for the twins. What are your names?"

"Sara," said one.

"Bea," said the other.

The girls bent over the babies. They tickled them. They played peek-a-boo and pat-a-cake with them. They exclaimed over their outfits.

"I can't wait until I can baby-sit," said Bea.

"It's the best job in the world," I replied.

"Is it ever hard?" Sara asked.

"Hard? Nah," I said, completely forgetting about the times Jamie Newton refused to go to sleep, and the day Jenny Prezzioso ran a fever of 104° and I had to call an ambulance, and the many things that had been broken by Jackie Rodowsky, the Walking Disaster. "It's always fun," I added. "I can't wait until I have children of my own." Or better yet, a baby sister, I thought.

"The twins were *angels*," I told Dawn later that afternoon.

It was almost dinnertime. Dad and Sharon

38

had not yet returned from work. Dawn and I had finished tossing a salad and had just stuck a casserole in the oven. It was some vegetarian thing Sharon had concocted. I didn't ask what was in it. I have found that it's better not to know.

"Rose and Ricky are pretty sweet," agreed Dawn.

"They didn't even *cry* today. Not even when I changed them."

"Babies are wonderful."

"I know. I don't understand why Dad and Sharon won't have one. I thought that was supposed to be part of a marriage. Look how badly Watson and Kristy's mom wanted a baby after they got married."

"Would you want a little brother or a little sister?" asked Dawn.

I hesitated. "I know I'm supposed to say I don't care as long as the baby is healthy, but, well, I would sort of like another sister," I said. "She would be so much fun to dress up. We could buy her jewelry and barrettes and some of those headbands — you know, the stretchy ones."

Dawn sat in a kitchen chair and said dreamily, "What would you want to name our sister . . . or brother?"

"I don't know about a brother, but I think a beautiful name for a girl is Tara. Or Charity.

Or Bea. Isn't Bea cute? I met a little girl today named Bea. Maybe Will would be nice for a boy."

"I think Dawn and Mary Anne are lovely names."

I jumped a mile, then whirled around to see who had spoken. It was Sharon. Dawn and I had been lost in some other world, and we hadn't heard our parents come home.

"Are you two talking about babies again?" asked Dad.

"Yes," I replied.

I couldn't bring myself to say anything more, but luckily Dawn jumped into the conversation. "We've noticed a pattern," she said. "People get married, then they have babies. Or they adopt babies or children."

"Not everyone," said Sharon. "Besides, between Richard and me we already have three children. And a cat."

"But don't the two of you want to have a baby together?" I asked.

"No," Sharon answered gently. "Not at this point in our lives."

"We're happy just the way we are," added Dad.

His voice carried that final note, the one that means, "End of discussion." The one that means, "I don't want to hear another word about it."

40

Dawn got the message, too. "Dinner's almost ready," she said.

So we ate dinner. No one said anything further about babies. But I couldn't stop *thinking* about them. Especially what to name a baby. I doodled in the margin of my math homework that evening: Tara, Lizzie, Margaret, Tara, Adele, Tara, Frannie, Tara, Charity, Bea . . .

CHAPTER 5

When Logan and I had worked out our finances for Modern Living class, we'd drawn a bunch of pretty negative conclusions: apartment rents were much higher than we'd expected; food was expensive; everything was expensive. And we could not yet be financially independent.

"What are we supposed to say in class tomorrow?" Logan asked. "Somehow, I have the feeling that 'we can't afford anything' isn't what Mrs. Boyden wants to hear. We could have told her that without doing *any* homework."

So Logan and I had written a two-page paper outlining how much money we earn, comparing the rents of different-sized apartments, and trying to figure out what percent of someone's salary should be spent on rent alone, and therefore how much we would need to earn to afford even the tiniest little apartment.

We made four professional-looking graphs, too. (We used Magic Markers, colored dots, rulers, even a protractor.)

Guess what. The day those homework assignments were due, we never even discussed them. We walked into our Modern Living classroom to find Mrs. Boyden sitting at her desk, her hands clasped in front of her. On the desk was a carton of eggs, the lid open. Mrs. Boyden said nothing as we filed into the room.

Something was going to happen.

"Logan," I dared to whisper, "do you think Mrs. Boyden is angry at our class? Did we do something wrong?"

Logan shrugged. "Beats me."

To be on the safe side, I handed in our homework assignment. I laid it silently on the edge of our teacher's desk. The other kids watched, then did the same thing.

When we were all seated quietly, Mrs. Boyden got to her feet. She smiled. "Congratulations," she said. "You have all become parents."

"Huh?" said Shawna.

"You've been married for awhile," Mrs. Boyden continued, "and now you have had babies. Congratulations."

I noticed a lot of confused faces in the room.

Mrs. Boyden indicated the carton of eggs.

"Your children," she said. "When I call your names, please come to the front of the room and receive your egg. Logan Bruno and Mary Anne Spier."

Feeling both confused and self-conscious, Logan and I made our way to Mrs. Boyden's desk. She held out an egg, which Logan accepted (because my hand was sort of shaking). When she didn't say anything else, we returned to our seats.

Pair by pair, the other kids were given eggs also. While Logan waited for everyone to sit down, he played with our egg. He placed it in the center of his desk, tapped it, sent it rolling, then caught it just before it sailed over the edge.

"Each of you now has a child," Mrs. Boyden announced, closing the lid on the carton. "The eggs are your children. For the next few weeks you are to treat the eggs as you would infants."

At that moment, Logan had just rolled our egg to the edge of his desk again. He caught it in a hurry. He handed it to me.

"Your babies," Mrs. Boyden was saying, "must be fed regularly, clothed, taken to the doctor, and especially, watched over. Just as you would never leave a human infant alone, you must never leave your egg alone. Someone must be available to care for it at all times.

You will be in charge of your egg-children for a month. At the end of four weeks, a paper will be due. I will expect you to write about your experiences, any problems you encountered, the solutions to those problems, and so forth. We'll talk more about the papers later this week. By the way, as parents you are responsible for your children, starting right now. Of course, I won't be able to see that your babies are cared for when you're out of school, so everyone is on his or her honor this month. Every eighth-grader will become a parent to an egg, and I trust you to keep an eye on each other. Only you can make the honor system work."

(Behind me, someone whispered, "Funny, I thought only we could prevent forest fires." Someone else giggled. Mrs. Boyden didn't notice.)

"Any questions?" our teacher asked.

As you can imagine, nearly everybody raised a hand.

"Shawna?" said Mrs. Boyden.

"Do we really have to take our eggs to the doctor?" she asked. "I might feel sort of silly. Like, what will the pediatrician think?"

Mrs. Boyden closed her eyes momentarily. "No, you don't actually have to take your egg to a doctor. But you are going to be a mother for a month, so I expect you to know when

45

and why your child might need to see a doctor. Remember to plan for checkups."

Logan nudged me. "How are we supposed to feed these eggs?" he asked.

I shrugged.

Shawna raised her hand again and spoke without waiting to be called on. "About food — " she began to say.

"No, you do not need to prepare food and pretend to feed your egg," Mrs. Boyden broke in. "Let me explain the project in more detail. When you leave this room at the end of the period, either you or your partner — your spouse — must watch over your child every moment. You wouldn't leave an infant unattended, so do not stash your egg in your locker during school hours. The egg will accompany you to classes. You must also tend to your egg after school and at night."

"Hey, what about after-school sports?" exclaimed a boy in the front row. "I can't watch an egg while I'm at baseball practice."

"Ask your wife to watch your child, then," said Mrs. Boyden.

"But I take piano lessons," spoke up the wife. She hesitated, then added, "I guess I could bring the egg with me."

Mrs. Boyden nodded. "That would be an acceptable solution, as long as you keep your eye on the baby throughout the lesson."

Mrs. Boyden mentioned some facts about babies. Not everyone was aware, for example, that infants cannot hold their own bottles. "What does that tell you about feeding your baby?" asked Mrs. Boyden.

"I guess we have to be *with* our egg at mealtimes," spoke up Trevor Sandbourne. "The baby can't eat by itself."

"Right. In fact, you need to *hold* the egg," pointed out Mrs. Boyden. "Infants can't sit up, either. Understand?" We nodded. "One last thing," our teacher went on, glancing at the clock. "From here on in, I would like you to refer to your children *as* children, rather than as eggs." Mrs. Boyden didn't explain this — the bell rang just as she finished her sentence — so I didn't have a chance to ask her *why* we weren't supposed to call our eggs eggs.

Around me, my classmates were getting to their feet. But not Logan. He turned to me with this incredible horrified expression on his face. Then he looked at our egg. I mean, our child. It was resting on my desk inside a little barricade I had created with my notebook, pocketbook, and two textbooks. For the time being it was safe, but —

"We can't carry that, um . . . we can't carry *that* around all day," said Logan, pointing at our child.

"Just what I was thinking," I answered. "But we have to."

"Yeah. Okay. Where will it be safe? In my backpack?"

"Not the way you sling that thing around. I'll put our child in my purse. She'll be safe there."

"Are you sure she won't suffocate? And how do you know it's a girl?"

"I don't. I just want a girl. And she won't suffocate. My bag doesn't close, see?" (My purse was a big woven bag. It was great for school because I could toss lots of stuff into it, and I didn't have to worry about zipping or unzipping it all day.)

"Okay," said Logan uncertainly.

"Hey, come on, this is going to be fun," I told him. I was standing up, settling our daughter in my purse.

"But what about gym? You and I have gym at the same time now. What are we going to do with her then? I'll be playing baseball. I can't bring her out on the field with me. It's too hot. Plus, I'd probably sit on her."

"Don't panic," I said, although I felt a teensy bit panicky myself. "I'll be doing aerobics in my gym class. I'll bring my bag with me and leave it where I can see it. She'll be fine."

"All right. I guess I'm just a nervous father."

"Well, relax. You're around kids all the time.

You're great with them. Pretend you're baby-sitting or something."

Logan relaxed. He looked fondly at our child, now nestled on a wad of Kleenex in my purse. "Maybe we should name her," he suggested.

"Yes, but not now, dear. We're going to be late for our next class." I picked up my books and slipped my purse over my shoulder.

Logan peered worriedly inside the bag. "Take care of our child," he said. "Be particularly careful during gym. Why don't you give her to me at lunch and I'll watch her for the rest of the day?"

"Oh, no," I said. "You are not putting our daughter in your backpack. This afternoon we'll get together and figure out a way to carry her around. I don't mind watching her today."

I had thought I might feel silly worrying about our child all day. I mean, how was I supposed to explain to my gym teacher that I needed to keep my purse nearby during aerobics so that I could baby-sit for an egg? But of course I wasn't the only student with that problem. A bunch of other girls who had also attended their Modern Living classes earlier that day were in the same situation. And I saw a couple of them just set their eggs on the floor and leave them. How would they be able to tell them apart at the end of class?

"Logan!" I exclaimed, when I met him in the cafeteria at lunchtime. "We have to mark our baby or something. What if she got lost? We wouldn't be able to tell her from any other egg. I mean, baby."

"This afternoon we'll paint her with food coloring," said Logan. "It's painless *and* nontoxic. You have to think of those things."

I nodded. "Listen, I'm sure she's hungry by now. Why don't you eat while I feed her? Then I'll eat while you finish feeding her. We should probably feed her again at . . ."

CHAPTER 6

Tuesday

When I accepted the job with the Papadakis' kids, I expected to baby-sit for just three children—Linny, Hannie, and Sari. I mean, the Papadakises only have three children. But I ended up bringing a fourth with me. My new son, Izzy the egg. My husband, Alan Gray, wanted to watch Izzy after school, but he wouldn't have been able to watch him in the evening, so I just brought Izzy home with me that afternoon, and at 3:45, carried him across the street to the Papadakises'. I think Izzy kind of confused the kids, but what would you expect?

W ell, of all things. Alan Gray has been Kristy's enemy (okay, her pest) for as long as I can remember. And who does she wind up marrying in her Modern Living class? Alan. How unfair.

How unfortunate. Kristy had a cow.

But that was on the day they got married. On the day they became parents, Kristy changed her mind about Alan. He turned out to be a pretty good father. First of all, he named Izzy.

"A son called Izzy," he had said dreamily to Kristy as he'd held his child for the first time.

"Izzy?" repeated Kristy. "What kind of name is that? Especially for a boy. I never heard of a boy named Izzy."

"It's short for, um . . ."

"It's short for Isabelle or Isadora or Elizabeth," said Kristy.

"Oh, it must be short for some boy's name," said Alan offhandedly. "Anyway, don't you think it's a nice name?"

"It *is* sort of cute," Kristy had agreed, pleased that Alan was at least taking an interest in the project.

By Tuesday, the day of Kristy's job at the Papadakises', both she and Alan were taking more than a little interest in Izzy. They had fixed this elaborate "environment" for him in a shoe box. The box was lined with pieces of flannel so Izzy would always be comfortable. The sides of the box were covered with felt so Izzy wouldn't hurt himself if he bumped into a wall. Alan had placed a tiny music box in the environment so Izzy would feel comforted and develop an appreciation for music. And Kristy had stuck tiny charts and pictures on the felt so Izzy's learning cells would be stimulated. She claimed she read aloud to him at night, but I don't know.

Also, unlike a lot of the couples in Modern Living, Kristy and Alan fought over who got to take their child home after school (as opposed to who got *stuck* with him after school). They were conscientious parents. Which is why Kristy never even considered leaving Izzy at her house while she went to the Papadakises'. Of *course* he went along with her.

The Papadakis kids are good friends of Kristy's younger brothers and sisters. Linny, who's nine, plays with David Michael. Hannie, who's seven, is one of Karen's two best friends. And Sari, the little one, sometimes plays with Emily. Kristy and the kids are pals. So Kristy decided that her first order of baby-sitting business should be to explain Izzy to them.

As Mrs. Papadakis backed down the driveway, Kristy sat at the kitchen table with Linny and Hannie. Sari, who had just woken up from a nap, was sitting sleepily in her high chair.

Kristy placed Izzy's environment on the table. She pointed to her son. "This," she said, "is Izzy Thomas-Gray."

"That egg?" replied Linny, after a moment's hesitation.

"Well, yes," answered Kristy. "Only he isn't — "

"*He?*" interrupted Linny.

" — he isn't just an egg," Kristy continued. "He's my son."

"You mean your pre*tend* son . . . don't you?" asked Hannie. She peered into the shoe box and stared at Izzy.

"Well, yes. My pretend son," Kristy agreed. Then she tried to explain Mrs. Boyden's Modern Living project to the kids.

"Okay, so you're pretend-married," said Linny, "and this egg is your pretend son. And you're baby-sitting for him, plus us. Right?"

"Right."

"Where is Izzy's food?" asked Hannie.

"The food is pretend, too," Kristy answered. "I just have to spend time with Izzy as *if* I were feeding him. Kind of like when you play with your dolls. You don't give them real food. Only with Izzy I have to remember to feed him every day, as often as — "

Ring, ring!

Linny bounded to his feet and made a grab for the phone. "I'll get it!" he cried. He picked up the receiver and said politely, "Hello, Papadakises' residence. Who's calling, please? . . . For Kristy? . . . Okay." Linny held the phone toward Kristy. "For you. I think it's your pretend husband."

"Hello?" said Kristy. "Alan? What's up?"

"I'm just checking on Izzy," he replied. "I was sitting here thinking about him, and . . . Is everything okay?"

"Oh, sure. Fine. Izzy's napping."

"Napping? Shouldn't he be eating? I don't think he eats enough. We don't want him to get scrawny."

"Alan, trust me. He's fine," said Kristy. "Um, except for — "

"WHAT?" exclaimed Alan. "Except for what?"

"He seems kind of nervous here."

"I thought he was asleep."

"He is now. But when we first got to the Papadakises', he was really shy."

"Well, you know, new faces."

"Yeah, but I'm concerned that he's not socializing right."

Kristy and Alan discussed Izzy's social development. They talked for quite awhile. They talked for so long that the kids became bored, and Linny lifted Sari out of her high chair, nudged Kristy, and whispered loudly, "We're going to the playroom."

"Okay," Kristy answered distractedly. Ten minutes later, she finished her conversation with Alan, hung up the phone, and headed for the kids' playroom. Halfway there she realized she was without Izzy, and she dashed back to the kitchen. The table was empty. Had Izzy been in the kitchen when Kristy finished her phone conversation? She couldn't remember. She glanced around the room, decided he wasn't in it, and headed for the playroom again, calling, "Linny? Hannie?"

"Yeah?" Linny called back.

"Do you have Izzy?"

"Huh?"

"I said, 'Do you have Izzy?' " By then, Kristy had reached the playroom. The first thing she saw was Izzy's environment. The box was on Hannie's small coloring table. "Never mind," said Kristy. She ran for the box.

It was empty.

I mean, it was empty of Izzy. Everything else was there — the flannel, the cell-stimulating pictures, the music box. Only Izzy was missing.

"Where is he? Where's Izzy?" cried Kristy with a gasp.

"Hey, funny!" exclaimed Linny. "Good joke. Get it? Where *is he?* Where's *Izzy?*" He laughed loudly.

Hannie began to laugh, too. "Where Izzy? Where Izzy?" she sang.

Even Sari laughed and joined in.

"This isn't funny, you guys," said Kristy, her heart pounding. "Izzy is like my baby. Remember? I'm responsible for him. Who brought his box in here? Linny?"

Linny's smile had faded. "Yeah, I did," he answered. "You were busy talking on the phone, and I thought Izzy might want to see the playroom."

"Okay." Kristy tried to calm down. "You brought his box in here? Then what? Did you take Izzy out of it?"

"Very, very gently," Hannie answered for her brother. Then she added, "*Very* gently. Honest. Cross my heart."

"I believe you," said Kristy. "Just tell me where you put Izzy."

Hannie frowned. She looked at Linny, who was frowning, too. "Linny was holding onto Izzy tightly and he walked — "

"How tightly?" Kristy interrupted.

"Not *that* tightly," said Linny.

"Linny showed Izzy around the playroom," Hannie continued. "He showed him the bookshelf and Sari's rocking horse and the art cupboard and the trucks and cars, and then . . ."

"Yeah?" prompted Kristy.

"I think he stopped to look at his collection of bottle caps."

"Oh, that's right," agreed Linny. "So I put Izzy on the floor and, um, that's all I remember. Until you came in."

"Everybody, spread out and search!" yelped Kristy.

"Hmm. If I were an egg, where would I go?" muttered Linny.

"How about the refrigerator?" suggested Hannie.

She and Linny got the giggles. While Kristy tossed aside books and toys and sweaters, looking for her missing son, Hannie and Linny cracked jokes and laughed helplessly.

"Maybe Izzy is off looking for Humpty Dumpty," said Hannie.

"Egg-sactly!" cried Linny. "Or maybe he had a great fall."

"Egg-cellent," said Hannie.

"I hope nobody found Izzy and then . . . cooked him and ate him," added Linny. "That would set a bad egg-zample."

By that time, Kristy was no longer listening to Hannie and Linny. "Come on, Sari. You'll help me, won't — Hey, Sari, what are you doing?" Kristy knelt beside Sari, who was squatting on the floor. At her feet was a doll's blanket. Sari was patting it and saying, "Baby, baby."

Kristy poked the blanket. Then she pulled at it. Inside was Izzy. "Oh, thank heaven! You're safe!" cried Kristy. "It's okay, Linny, Hannie. I found him. Guess what. Sari was taking care of Izzy for us."

"Darn. No more egg-citement," said Linny.

Even Kristy couldn't help laughing. "Linny!" she exclaimed.

"Sorry," he said. "It's just . . . I don't know. Your *son?* An egg named Izzy? I never heard of anything like that."

"Egg-straordinary, isn't it?" said Kristy. And then she replaced Izzy in his safe environment.

She decided not to tell Alan what had happened.

CHAPTER 7

Our daughter had a name. She went without one for four days while Logan and I argued over what to call her. I was holding out for Tara, but Logan didn't like the name. He wanted to call her Sally, which I thought was much too plain. Finally we compromised.

We named our child Samantha.

I thought Samantha was almost as beautiful as Tara, and that Sammie was an adorable nickname. Logan liked Sammie, too, because it sounded like Sally.

We fixed a wicker basket for Sammie and lined it with scraps of pink fabric. The day we had been given Sammie, we had painted pink flowers on her with food coloring. The day we named her, we added this:

S

"Now we'll always be able to recognize her," said Logan.

"*And* she's beautiful," I added. "Our beautiful daughter."

As soon as Sammie's basket was prepared, Logan took on more than his share of the work in caring for our daughter. He took her home with him almost every afternoon. He carried her around school as often as possible.

He was a natural father.

Of course, he couldn't care for Sammie *all* the time, though. And one morning he met me in school, basket in hand, and said, "Just as I was leaving the house, Hunter reminded me that I promised to take him and Kerry to the playground this afternoon. I'm worried about taking Sammie with me. I don't want her to get too much sun."

"I'll take her," I said. "I'm baby-sitting for Rose and Ricky after school, but that shouldn't be a problem. It'll probably be easier for me to take care of three infants than for you to take care of one infant and two active kids. I mean, the twins can't walk yet. How much harder could three babies be than two?"

I found out at the Salems' house. Three could be plenty harder than two, and even two could be . . . a nightmare.

The bad dream began shortly after Mrs. Salem left the house, when Ricky woke up from his nap.

He woke up crying.

I had been sitting in the kitchen with Sammie's basket in my lap (while supposedly I gave Sammie a bottle), when I heard snuffles and tears from the twins' bedroom.

"I'm coming!" I called gently, so as not to wake the other twin.

I stood up. "Sorry, Sammie," I said. "You'll have to finish your bottle later." I knew that wasn't quite fair. If Sammie had been a real infant, I would have had to figure out how to feed her *and* rush upstairs. As it was, I had to bring her with me.

I entered the babies' room and found a very unhappy Ricky. He was sitting at one end of the crib, wailing, tears streaming down his face.

"Shh, Ricky, shh," I whispered. "What's the matter?"

I set Sammie on the changing table and picked up Ricky. I rocked him and walked him around the room until I realized that Rose was stirring. Then I took him into the hallway —

and realized I'd left Sammie behind. An infant should never be left on a changing table un-attended. So I went back to retrieve her, and Ricky's cries woke Rose, who also began to cry.

"Hey, come on, you guys. I can't hold both of you," I said, remembering at the same time that I hadn't finished feeding Sammie. Then the thought occurred to me that the twins were probably hungry. Also, that they could hold their own bottles. So I settled the babies in their high chairs and handed each one a bottle. Perfect. They could feed themselves while I fed Sammie.

Well, that worked in theory. In reality, Rose continued to fuss, so I held Sammie in my lap and fed Rose myself. This arrangement lasted until Ricky threw his bottle on the floor.

I stopped what I was doing, picked it up, handed it to him, and returned to Rose. Ricky threw down the bottle again. I decided Sam-mie had eaten enough and stood between the twins, holding Rose's bottle with my right hand and Ricky's with my left.

When the bottles were empty, I stepped back and examined the babies.

"You guys look simply delightful," I told them. (I didn't mean it.)

They were far from the beautiful babies I'd dressed on my last sitting job. They were wearing rumpled T-shirts and damp diapers. Their cheeks were tearstained and their chins were milk-covered.

"Time to fix you up," I said decisively.

With difficulty, I returned Sammie, Rose, and Ricky to the twins' room. I set Rose in her crib, Sammie on the windowsill, and Ricky on the changing table. I removed Ricky's wet diaper.

"Wah!" he wailed.

He cried the *entire* time I changed him.

"You aren't getting sick, are you?" I asked. I felt his forehead. No temperature. And his appetite had seemed fine. When he was dry and powdered, I returned him to his crib and placed Rose on the table. She cried mightily while I changed her.

"Having a bad day?" I said to the twins.

They stared at me from tear-filled eyes.

At least their bottoms were dry.

"How about a walk?" I suggested. Walks are good for stopping tears.

I removed two lovely outfits from the closet. For Rose, a white ruffled dress with matching panties and a hat, and her pink shoes. For Ricky, a frog jumpsuit with a matching shirt and hat, and his tiny high-topped sneakers.

The babies eyed all those clothes warily. They turned on the tears before I'd even so much as lifted Ricky's arms. In the end, they left the house wearing clean T-shirts, fresh pants, and socks. No earrings or frills for Rose. No hat for either of them. Not even shoes. At least they'd whittled down their crying to sniffles and hiccups. They weren't happy, but they were quiet.

I hung Sammie's basket over a handle of the double stroller. Then I set out with the three babies. For awhile, they were quiet. They seemed content. I managed to convince myself that Sammie had had enough to eat and I hadn't neglected her *too* badly. I relaxed.

And Rose began bumping back and forth in her seat and making these awful whiny noises. She wasn't exactly crying, but —

Time for a distraction technique. "What a beautiful day!" I exclaimed. I pointed to the sky. "Look, I see a bird. Bird."

"Ba!" said Rose.

"That's right. Bird. And there's a cloud."

We stopped next to a garden. "Ooh, pretty flowers," I said.

Ricky reached for a tulip, got a grip on the stem, and pulled.

The plant uprooted, sending dirt flying.

"Ricky!" I cried. I whirled around and looked at the house beyond the garden. What if someone had seen us? "Ricky!" I said again.

"No, no, no!" I took the flower from him and dropped it in the garden. I tried to bury it under some leaves and mulch. Then for good measure, I said "No!" to Ricky once more.

Both babies, looking bewildered, burst into tears.

Uh-oh. "Sorry, Ricky. I'm sorry," I said. "Rose, I'm sorry. I didn't mean to shout. But Ricky, you can't go around pulling up plants. That flower isn't yours. It belongs to someone else." (Like he could really understand me.)

I wheeled the stroller away quickly and hurried down the sidewalk with my cargo of crying babies. If Logan had been at home, I *might* have phoned him and asked him to come get Sammie. But I coped as well as I could.

"That was a nightmare, all right," Dawn said that evening, when I described my job at the Salems' to her.

"Yeah. I guess it could have been worse, though."

"How? If the house had burned down?"

"No, if, um, well, I'm not sure. I mean, this just wasn't realistic, that's all. I don't usually baby-sit for three infants at once. I have to admit, I thought the job wouldn't be bad since the babies can't walk. I should have realized how silly that is. I still have only one pair of hands, and most people take care of just one baby at a time. Anyway, nothing bad actually happened this afternoon. The babies were fussy, but you have to expect that. I still want a little sister, don't you? A real one, I mean. Not an egg one. Even a little brother would be okay.''

"Yeah, I still want a sister or brother," Dawn replied. "And you know what came in the mail today?"

"What?"

"The Kumbel catalog."

"The *Kum*bel catalog?" I shrieked. The Kumbel catalog sells *every*thing. Dawn knows what my favorite section is. Baby supplies and furnishings. "Where is it?"

"In my room. I'll go get it." Dawn dashed down the hallway, then returned to my bedroom, clutching the fat catalog.

I found the baby section in about three seconds. "Aw, look!" I exclaimed. "Look at that crib. It would be perfect for a girl *or* a boy. White with yellow stars and a moon."

"It *is* adorable," agreed Dawn. "And we could get that matching dresser and rocking chair. A yellow-and-white baby's room would be so cute."

"If Dad and Sharon had a baby," I said thoughtfully, "I guess you and I would end up sharing a room again." (We had tried that once. It had not worked.) "My room would become the baby's room."

"No, the baby could have Jeff's room, I think."

"Oh, whatever. Hey, look at *that!* A baby's lamp with a stars-and-moon shade. Tara would *have* to have that."

"Tara?" said three voices.

Darn it. Dad and Sharon had overheard us talking again.

"Yeah. Our . . . baby sister?" I ventured.

"No," said Dad.

"No way," said Sharon.

"Double darn," I replied.

CHAPTER 8

Ten people attended the next meeting of the Baby-sitters Club. Seven humans and three infants. (Okay, three eggs.) Sammie, Izzy, and Bobby.

Bobby was Stacey's little boy. (Claudia's child was over at his father's house.) He lived in a plastic mixing bowl. His father was Austin Bentley, a friend of Stacey's and Claudia's. Austin sometimes invites one or the other of them to school dances or to parties, but he isn't their boyfriend. (A good thing, too, because I think he'd have trouble choosing between them.) The three of them are just regular friends.

Claud had fixed a sort of nursery in her room. The nursery was an area on her dresser on which sat Sammie in her basket, Izzy in his shoe box environment, and Bobby in his mixing bowl. She had placed pillows on the floor around the dresser in case one of the babies fell off.

"Why don't you just put the babies on the floor?" asked Mal practically. "Then they wouldn't be able to fall."

"Too drafty," Kristy answered.

"So how are your kids doing?" Jessi inquired politely.

"Sammie's fine," I said, "but Logan —

"Order! Come to order, please!" said Kristy.

(I checked the official club timepiece. Sure enough. Five-thirty.)

My friends and I straightened up. We adjusted ourselves.

"Any club business?" our president wanted to know.

No one answered her. So I said simply, "Logan is hogging Sammie. Lately, he is almost always taking care of her." Tears welled in my eyes. "This is the first time I've brought her home after school since the day I baby-sat for the Tragedy Twins."

Stacey giggled. "You mean Ricky and Rose?"

"Yeah." I couldn't even laugh at my own joke.

The phone rang and Claud picked it up. "Hello, Baby-sitters Club. . . . Mm-hmm, mm-hmm. . . . In Karen Brewer's class? . . . *Oh.* . . . Thursday afternoon? I'll check and call you right back." Claud hung up and said, "That was someone named Mr. Gianelli. He said his son is in Karen's class at Stoneybrook Academy."

"Gianelli," repeated Kristy. "He must be Bobby's father."

"Right," said Claud. "The Gianellis have two kids, Bobby and his little sister, Alicia. They need a sitter on Thursday afternoon."

I looked at the appointment pages in the record book. "You can do it, Stace," I said. "Want the job?"

"Sure."

Claud phoned Mr. Gianelli back while I scribbled in the BSC record book. I love filling in those blank spaces.

"I don't know why you want to spend so much time with an egg," Stacey said to me. She brushed her hair out of her eye.

I gasped. "Sammie is my *daugh*ter!" I exclaimed.

Stacey made a face. "Honestly, Mary Anne."

"You heard what Mrs. Boyden said."

"Yeah, yeah. And I'm doing the project. So's Austin. We're very fair and careful. We each take care of Bobby exactly half the time. One day I bring him home, one day Austin brings him home. But what a pain. I don't think I have time for Modern Living class.

Always having to stop and think about feeding Bobby or giving him a bath or something. On Monday I took him shopping with Mom and me. I figured a baby would need new undershirts and diapers and stuff pretty often. So I lugged the mixing bowl around four baby departments while Mom shopped for fun things, like books and presents. All I saw were baby thermometers and baby minders and baby sneakers and baby toys and baby bottles and baby blankets. Babies sure need a lot of equipment. I never even had a chance to check out clothes for *me*."

"Oh, but buying baby things is fun," I spoke up. I was thinking about the Kumbel catalog.

"For five minutes," said Stacey.

"Well, anyway, I — I — " (I was trying to think of a nice way to say I didn't agree with Stacey.) "I guess I don't mind shopping for baby things. And I *still* wish Logan wouldn't hog Sammie."

From her place on the floor, Mal tried to hide a giggle.

"What's so funny?" asked Dawn.

"Mary Anne keeps saying Logan is *hogging* Sammie. And 'hogging' makes me think of bacon. And Sammie is an egg. Get it? Bacon and eggs?" Mallory snorted with laughter.

Jessi began to laugh, too.

But us five older club members remained

serious. After a few moments, Claud said, "You guys don't understand. You aren't parents yet."

Mal and Jessi quieted down.

We took a few phone calls. Then Kristy got up from the director's chair, crossed the room to the dresser, and peeked into Izzy's box. "I think Izzy is getting spoiled," she said.

"Too much attention?" I asked.

"No, I mean I think he's spoiling. Smell him."

Kristy is forever asking me to smell disgusting things. I don't know why she thinks I'll do it.

"No, thanks," I replied.

But brave Dawn stood up and sniffed around in the box. "I don't smell anything," she said. "You're making up worries."

"I am not," Kristy replied. However, she sat down again.

"You guys? What's being married like?" asked Jessi.

"Yeah, what's it like?" echoed Mal.

"Well," Stacey began after a moment, "I don't know what to compare it to. But a lot of it is communicating. With your husband or wife. You have to be able to talk about who's going to watch the baby when, and who has to remember to do which things with the baby."

"And you have to agree on stuff," added Kristy. "And trust your husband. That's really important. You have to trust him."

"Being married is expensive," I added.

"Nobody has said anything about love," pointed out Jessi.

The room grew silent.

"Yeah, aren't you supposed to be in love?" asked Mal.

"I guess that *would* make things easier," said Stacey slowly. "If I were actually in love with Austin, I'd want to spend more time with him. And I'd want our child to spend more time with us. Maybe being married wouldn't seem like *quite* so much work."

"I know what you mean," I said. "Marriage would still be difficult and expensive. But, boy, if I didn't love Logan — Um, if I didn't *like* him a lot — " (I was blushing.)

Dawn smiled. "You can say 'love,' Mary Anne."

"Okay. If I didn't love him, I could never be married to him and take care of Sammie with him. It's hard enough when we do love each other. . . . Oh, I almost forgot. I have to feed — "

The phone rang. Jessi picked it up. "Logan? Sure, hang on a sec." Jessi handed the phone to me. "It's your husband."

"Hi, dear," I said.

"Hi. Did you feed Sammie?"

"I was just about to."

"Okay. By the way, is Claudia's room warm enough?"

"Yes." Logan reminded me of Kristy and Alan.

"Maybe you should add a little blanket to the basket."

"But it's almost seventy degrees outside . . . *dear*," I said. "Sammie is fine. Or she will be after I feed her."

Logan let me hang up and feed Sammie. Kristy fed Izzy, and Stacey fed Bobby. "You know," said Kristy, "if we really had to feed babies, we'd have to stop and fix formula. That would take even more time. I think we're getting off easy."

"I *still* wish Logan would let me take care of Sammie more often," I said. "Sometimes I think he doesn't trust me."

"Oh, he's just being overprotective," said Claud.

There seemed to be a lot of that going around.

"Well, I think you guys should just feel lucky that you *don't* actually have babies," said Jessi. "That this is just a school project."

"And that it will be over in less than a month," added Mal. "I remember when my mom was pregnant with Claire. If she had been in school then, she would have had to drop out."

"Mallory. She had six *other* kids to care for," said Kristy.

"That's not what I mean. You don't know how tired you feel when you're pregnant. And you're even tireder after the baby comes. Busier, too."

Hmm. I wondered if Sharon could handle her job, as well as being "tireder" and busier than usual. Well, of course she could. Dawn and I would help her whenever she wanted. She would only have to do one third of the usual mothering. Now, if only she and Dad would just come to their senses.

CHAPTER 9

Thursday

Who knew an egg could be so scary? Well, maybe I should have known. When I was five I went through this phase during which I was terrified of pigeons for no good reason. Anyway, I sat for Bobby and Alicia Gianelli this afternoon, and Alicia... well, when she first saw my son she screamed. Mrs. Gianelli hadn't said anything about Alicia having an egg phobia, so I suppose it was the surprise of finding an egg underneath the washcloths in the mixing bowl. Maybe she expected a kitten or something. Plus, the egg's name was the same as her brother's. I guess that was confusing.

The Gianellis were new clients of the BSC. None of us had baby-sat for them before the afternoon of Stacey's job. Kristy knew Bobby slightly because he's in Karen's class at school. That was how the Gianellis had heard about the BSC. But basically they were uncharted territory. You know, a new experience.

Uncharted territories and new experiences make me nervous, but Stacey enjoys a good challenge. She was looking forward to her job at the Gianellis'. She adores meeting people, especially kids.

Stacey walked straight to the Gianellis' house after school. She ran up their front steps, stuck her finger out to ring the bell, and realized there was a piece of tape over it. (Over the bell, that is. Not over her finger.) To the left of the bell was a small sign that read, CHILD SLEEPING, PLEASE KNOCK.

Stacey knocked lightly on the door, and it was opened by this tall guy with a mustache. "Hi, I'm Mr. Gianelli," he whispered.

"I'm Stacey McGill," Stacey replied.

Mr. Gianelli ushered Stace inside, quietly explaining that Mrs. Gianelli was at work, Alicia was napping, and Bobby had not yet come home from school. "He takes the bus," said Mr. Gianelli in explanation. Then he noticed

Stacey's mixing bowl. "What's that?" he asked.

Stacey began to tell him about Mrs. Boyden and Modern Living, but Mr. Gianelli interrupted her. "Ah, the egg project," he said. "I know it well. I used to be a teacher. Good luck."

He gave Stacey some instructions, showed her where important things (like the first-aid kit) were kept, handed her a list of emergency phone numbers, then left to go to a meeting in Stamford.

Stacey sat at the kitchen table and waited for Bobby to come home or for Alicia to wake up. While she waited, she talked to her own Bobby, the one in the plastic mixing bowl.

"Pretend I'm feeding you," she said wearily to the egg. "By the way, you're going over to your father's house tonight instead of tomorrow. I can't take care of you tonight. I'm way behind in everything, thanks to — "

"Are you the baby-sitter?" asked a sleepy voice.

Stacey snapped her head around. She hadn't heard anyone enter the kitchen. Standing a few feet away, apparently keeping her distance, was a dark-haired, dark-eyed little girl with olive skin. She looked curiously from Stacey to the mixing bowl and back to Stacey.

"Hi!" Stacey said brightly. "Yes, I'm your sitter. My name is Stacey. Stacey McGill. I guess you're Alicia."

The girl nodded. Then she held up four fingers. "I'm this many," she added.

"I bet you just had your birthday."

Alicia nodded again. "What's in the bowl?" she asked. "What are you talking to?" She stepped closer to Stacey.

Stacey grinned. "I think you'll be surprised. Want to see?"

"Okay." Alicia peered into the bowl.

Stacey pulled back the washcloths. There was Bobby.

"Aughhh!" shrieked Alicia. She burst into tears.

"What's the matter?" exclaimed Stacey.

"I don't like that thing! Why do you have it with you?"

Stacey paused, trying to figure out what to tell Alicia. Before she had a chance to speak, the front door opened, then closed. "Bobby!" cried Alicia.

Bobby Gianelli hurtled himself into the kitchen and flung his knapsack on the floor. "I'm home!" he announced. "Hi, Alicia. Hi, baby-sitter."

Alicia was still crying. "Bobby, look in that bowl," she said, pointing.

Bobby took a look at Bobby. "Weird," he

said. He opened the refrigerator and removed a carton of milk. "Whose is it?"

"It's mine," Stacey answered. And then she did explain about the Modern Living project. "And you'll never guess what," she said finally.

"What?" asked Bobby. He and Alicia were seated at the table, facing Stacey. They looked at her seriously.

"His name is Bobby."

"That *egg's* name is Bobby?" said Bobby.

Stacey nodded. "Well, remember, I'm supposed to pretend it's my kid, not just an egg. And if he were my kid, I would have named him."

"Right," said Bobby. He set his empty glass in the sink.

"So, Bobby, what do you want to do today?" asked Stacey.

Bobby opened a cupboard and looked inside. He closed the cupboard. Then he knelt down and opened his knapsack.

"Bobby?" said Stacey again. (No answer.) "Bobby?"

"Are you talking to me?" asked Bobby. (Stacey nodded.) "Oh, sorry. I thought you were talking to your egg. What do I want to do today? I don't know. Play football, I guess, if the other kids will play. I better change into my uniform." Bobby left the kitchen. From halfway up the stairs to the second floor he called, "Can I bring Bobby with me?"

"You *are* Bobby!" replied Alicia.

"I think he means this Bobby," Stacey said, tapping the mixing bowl. "I'll see!" she called back. (She was thinking, No way.)

"Oh, good. Let Bobby take that egg," said Alicia, who was sitting as far from the bowl as possible, her eyebrows knitted.

"Don't you like Bobby?" asked Stacey.

"He's my brother!" replied Alicia.

"I mean the egg. Are you afraid of Bobby the egg?"

"Yes."

"Are you afraid of all eggs?"

"No."

"Then why are you afraid of Bobby?"

"I'm not. He's my — "

"Bobby the *egg!*"

"I never saw an egg in bed before."

"Pretend he's a baby, not an egg."

At that moment, Bobby the boy returned to the kitchen in his football uniform, which turned out to be a sweat shirt, a pair of jeans, and a bicycle helmet. "Okay, I'm ready," he said. "Is the egg?"

"Is *Bobby*," Alicia corrected him.

"What?" said Bobby.

"What?" said Stacey.

"Never mind," said Alicia.

"I'm ready to play football with the egg," said Bobby.

Yikes, thought Stacey. "Bobby," she said, "I have to take care of the egg. He belongs to me. Do you understand?"

"Sort of." Bobby left then, saying he would be across the street.

"Okay, Alicia, what do *you* want to do?" asked Stacey.

"Walk to the brook. But not with Bobby."

Stacey sighed. Then she saw that Alicia was truly frightened, so she called Austin Bentley and asked him to come pick up Bobby early. Luckily, he was at home. Later, after he and Bobby had left, Stacey and Alicia walked down the street to the little brook. Alicia sat on a sunny rock and tossed pebbles into the water. Stacey sat in a patch of dry grass and thought. What if Bobby had been her real child and she had had no husband to call on for help? she wondered. What did you do if you were a single parent and you were at work and your child got sick and the nurse called and said he should go home from school? What if you couldn't leave your job? Or what if you were at home and something happened to you and you simply needed help?

"I bet my mom is scared sometimes," Stacey said over the phone to me that night. "I bet she wonders about the 'what ifs.' Like what if she got a job and she was at work and I was at school and I went into a diabetic coma? Or what if something happened to *Mom* and no one could get in touch with my dad? I bet Mom worries a lot, Mary Anne."

"I think all parents do," I replied.

"But they probably feel a little safer if they aren't *single* parents."

"Mm. Maybe. Stace? Are you worried because you're the daughter of a divorced mom? And your dad doesn't live nearby? That would be okay. I used to worry more when my dad was single."

"Yeah. I worry sometimes." Stacey paused. "You know, this afternoon was kind of funny with the two Bobbies, and Alicia afraid of the egg and everything. But I decided something. I am going to wait until I'm *really old* before I have a human baby."

CHAPTER 10

Ever since we had our baby, Logan and I had spent very little time alone together. We hadn't been out — just the two of us — in ages. How many places can you easily take an infant to? I guess we *could* have taken Sammie to Pizza Express or the diner or the coffee shop, but it just didn't seem like a great idea. Anyway, Logan and I would have been busy feeding Sammie, holding her, and doing all those things you have to do to occupy an infant, and that would have sort of defeated the purpose.

But one Friday, at the end of Modern Living class, Logan said to me, "Mary Anne, I'd really like for us to go out tonight. I hate to leave Sammie behind, but . . . I don't know. I just want to go to a movie or something."

Considering how attached Logan had become to our daughter, this seemed like an especially nice idea. I think he was taking our

class project a little more seriously than anyone, except maybe Alan and Kristy. If I hadn't
known better, I might have thought he cared
more about Sammie than he did about me. So
a movie sounded like a terrific idea, and I told
him so. "Oh, Logan, awesome!" I exclaimed.
"I can't wait. And don't worry about Sammie.
I'll take care of everything."

"Great. I'll come to your house at six-thirty."

Ding-dong.
That evening, our doorbell rang promptly
at six-thirty. Dad and Sharon were upstairs
getting ready to go out to dinner. Dawn was
baby-sitting for Haley and Matt Braddock.

I was standing at the front door holding
Sammie in her basket.

When I let Logan inside, the first words out
of his mouth were, "What's Sammie doing?"
He took the basket from me.

"Sleeping?" I suggested.

"I mean, what's she doing *here?*"

"Coming with us," I answered. "We can't
leave her alone."

"Didn't you get a baby-sitter?"

I shook my head. "Dad and Sharon are
going out. Dawn's baby-sitting at the Brad-
docks'. I didn't want to ask any of them to
watch Sammie."

"Well, what about someone else? Claudia or someone?"

"Oh, Logan. Can't we just bring Sammie with us? We don't have time to find a sitter now. We'll miss the beginning of the movie."

"Bring an infant to the movie theater? No way."

But in the end, that was what we did.

I checked Sammie to make sure the identifying marks on her shell still showed up. Then I added a large scrap of flannel to her basket, since our movie theater begins using the air-conditioning around the middle of March, in order to keep the temperature at a pretty steady 45° year-round.

"When's she due for her next feeding?" Logan asked me, as we stood on a line stretching down the sidewalk.

"Right in the middle of the movie," I answered. "But that'll be okay. One of us will be holding her anyway."

"Yeah. One of us will."

Something in Logan's tone of voice made me glance at him and wonder exactly how our evening was going to go. But just then the doors to the theater opened, and we filed inside along with the rest of the crowd. I grew busy juggling Sammie, my pocketbook, and the extra sweaters I'd brought along. I forgot what Logan had said. And how he'd said it.

"Are you hungry?" Logan asked me, as we walked through the lobby.

"Sort of. Are you?"

"Starving. I didn't eat dinner. What do you want?"

"A small popcorn and a small diet Coke."

"Okay." Logan stepped up to the counter and said to the woman, "One small popcorn, one giant popcorn, one small diet Coke, one large diet Coke, and a large box of Peanut M&M's, please."

Well, not only did all that food cost a fortune, but the two of us couldn't carry it. Not with Sammie and the sweaters. We had to get one of those cardboard boxes like you get on trains, and then sort of hobble into the theater and down a darkened aisle.

"If we were really married and really on a budget," I said to Logan, as we looked for seats, "we could probably have paid our electricity bill with the money we spent on food and movie tickets tonight."

"I know."

"Just think if we had to pay a baby-sitter, too."

"I guess you have to splurge sometime," said Logan, but he looked as if he weren't sure he meant that.

The theater was becoming crowded. Even

so, I whispered to Logan, "I think we're going to need three seats tonight. We have so much stuff."

Luckily we found a row consisting of three empty seats. It was way over on the side of the theater, and kind of close to the front, but at least we'd found what we needed. I eased myself into the middle seat, and Logan sat on the aisle. I set Sammie in the third seat, the one by the wall. But she didn't weigh enough to hold the seat down.

It flipped back up, trapping Sammie and her basket between the seat and the seat back. "Yikes!" I cried.

Logan saw what had happened, but he was holding that flimsy box full of spilly sodas and popcorn. He needed both hands to carry it. Even so, he nearly dropped it. "Mary Anne!" he hissed.

"I'm *sorry*," I said crossly. I dropped my armload of sweaters and grabbed the handle of Sammie's basket with one hand and the seat with the other. I pushed the seat down and gingerly lifted the basket.

Sammie was safe inside.

"She's okay," I said to Logan.

"I knew this wasn't a good idea," he replied. "Okay. Now *hold* Sammie."

"I can't. I mean, I can't hold her *and* the popcorn *and* the soda. Just a sec." I pulled down the murderous seat again and placed the sweaters on it. "Do you want to give me your coat?" I asked Logan. (He actually likes the temperature in the movie theater.)

Logan put the tray of food on the floor, took off his coat, handed it to me, and picked up the food. Then I placed Sammie on Logan's coat, and he handed me my popcorn and soda. At last we were settled.

"Excuse me, is that seat taken?"

Logan and I glanced up. Standing at Logan's elbow was a tall man in a suit. He was looking at Sammie's seat with raised eyebrows.

"Well," said Logan.

"Well," I said.

The man checked his watch. "The movie's going to begin any minute now, and the theater is packed," he pointed out.

I thought about what might happen if I told the man the seat was occupied by an egg. The outcome didn't look good.

Logan must have been thinking the same thing, because he sighed and said, "No, it's not taken."

I gave Logan back his coat, which he sat on.

I put on one of the sweaters.

I sat on the others.

Then I put Sammie in my lap.

"Logan," I whispered as the lights began to

dim, "I can't hold Sammie and eat, too." (My food was on the floor.)

"Neither can I," Logan replied. "Plus, I have more food than you do."

"All right. I'm going to put Sammie's basket on the floor until I'm finished eating. She'll be okay there."

"Shhh!" hissed the man on the other side of me. He was the first person I had ever met who wanted to pay attention to the cartoon about not littering in the theater, and buying fresh popcorn at the concession stand, and being able to locate the exits in case of fire.

"Sorry," I replied.

"You can't put Sammie on the floor!" Logan whispered loudly.

"SHHH!"

"Sorry."

I put Sammie on the floor anyway. "She's right between my feet," I said to Logan. "If anyone takes her basket, I'll know about it."

"Excuse me," said the man, "are you two going to talk through the *entire* movie, or just this first portion?"

"Sorry," I said again.

But Logan said, "I think just this first portion." Only he said it so softly the man didn't hear him.

The movie turned out to be really good. It

was funny and exciting. I was glad for that. During the first half of the picture, Logan kept turning to me and grinning. He was relaxing. So was I.

Except for my right foot. It had gone numb from being held in the same position for so long. Sammie or no Sammie, I had to shift my legs. So I did. Then I reached down to check on her. I felt around inside the basket.

Sammie was gone.

I gasped.

"What's the matter?" asked Logan.

"Sammie's not in the basket," I said. My heart was pounding. Logan grabbed up the basket. Then *he* felt around inside it. "She must have fallen out!" he exclaimed, trying to whisper. "You let her fall out. You lost our daughter!"

"I did not!"

"You did too. I bet she's rolling around in the aisle somewhere."

Logan was half right. Sammie was rolling around, but she wasn't in the aisle. She was just under my seat. Except we didn't discover that until after Logan had panicked and called over an usher to shine his flashlight on the floor. I thought the man in the third seat would kill us.

When Sammie was nestled safely in her basket again, Logan said stiffly, "Maybe we should hard-boil her." Then he tugged at my elbow. "Come on. We're going now, Mary Anne."

"Fine," I replied.

"Good," said the man.

We carried our stuff to the lobby, threw away our trash, and struggled into our coats. Logan picked up Sammie's basket.

"*I'm* supposed to have her tonight!" I cried.

"No way. You almost lost her," said Logan. "Not that I really want to take care of her *again*. I'm always taking care of her."

"You mean you're always *taking* her. You never let me have her."

"Okay, then *you* take her tonight."

"Oh, no. You don't trust me. You just said so."

Logan didn't answer. He grabbed Sammie's basket. Then he went off to call his parents for a ride home, and I called my dad, and Logan and I went off in a huff.

CHAPTER 11

Tuesday

Well, my brothers and sisters did it again.

I don't know why that surprises you anymore, Mal.

I don't know why, either. But really... it's a good thing my parents are so tolerant. They'll have to buy another dozen eggs tomorrow.

Yeah. The kids were nice to Skip, though. I think they liked him.

Lucky for him.

What's that supposed to mean?

Nothing. Never mind. Come on, Dawn, we're way off track. We better finish this notebook entry. We have a meeting tomorrow.

On Tuesday night Mr. and Mrs. Pike went to Parents' Night at Stoneybrook Elementary School. Imagine what the evening is like for them. *Seven* of their kids are students at the school: Claire in kindergarten, Margo in second grade, Nicky in third, Vanessa in fourth, and the triplets in fifth. No wonder they stay for the full three hours the school is open. (When I went to SES, my dad could do Parents' Night in under an hour.)

While the Pikes visited SES, Mal and Dawn sat for Mal's younger brothers and sisters. Dawn left our house shortly after six-thirty. She left with her child, an egg named Skip. Skip lived in an empty Kleenex box, standard size. Dawn and her husband, this guy Aaron Albright, whom Dawn didn't like very much, hadn't fixed up the box except to line it with some paper towels to prevent Skip from injuring himself. (For the record, Dawn did *not* name Skip. Aaron did. Dawn said if she'd had her way, she would have named her son Douglas. She said Douglas is a good, strong name, and that Skip is what you'd name some little cartoon character, like maybe a young chicken wearing sneakers and a beanie.)

Dawn and Skip arrived at Mallory's just as Mr. and Mrs. Pike were getting ready to leave. Mal was trying to involve the triplets in helping her clean up the kitchen after dinner.

"Washing dishes is girls' work," Dawn heard Adam say.

"Adam," Mal replied, "there is no such thing as girls' work. But if there were, it would be called women's work."

"There is too *girls'* work," said Adam.

"Is there boys' work?" Mal asked him.

"Sure."

"What is it?"

"Shoveling snow."

"I can do that," said Mal.

"Mowing lawns."

"I can do that."

"Cleaning gutters."

"I can do that."

Adam turned away from his sister, looking pained. He couldn't win the argument, and he knew it. Luckily, when he turned around, he found a distraction. Dawn and the Kleenex box.

"Hi, everybody," said Dawn.

The youngest kids were still sitting at the kitchen table, dawdling over dishes of ice cream. Vanessa was sitting there, too, but a pad of paper lay in front of her. She was scribbling on it, probably composing a new poem. Mal was at the sink, and the triplets were hovering around the doorway, trying to escape the cleanup process.

Adam spotted Skip's box immediately. "What's that?" he asked.

"What's what?" answered Dawn, which only goes to show how accustomed my friends and I had grown to lugging around mixing bowls and Kleenex boxes and stuff.

"That box," said Adam.

"Yeah, what is it? It's too small to be a Kid-Kit," added Margo.

"Oh, it's Skip, my egg," said Dawn wearily. "I'm supposed to pretend he's my baby. You know, feed him and everything."

"Feed an *egg?*" asked Jordan.

"Well, not really." Dawn described the Modern Living experiment with a little help from Mallory.

The Pike kids were so interested that they barely noticed when their parents left for the elementary school. " 'Bye," they called vaguely.

"Dawn? How long will you be married to Aaron?" asked Vanessa.

"Hey, is your name Dawn Albright now?" Claire wanted to know.

"Yeah, do we have to call you Mrs. Albright?" Nicky giggled.

"Oh, I hope not," said Dawn, but she was smiling. "Even if we had really, really, *really* gotten married, I wouldn't have changed my name. I like my name. I will always be Dawn Schafer."

Byron was looking into the Kleenex box for about the ninety-fifth time. "Your baby is naked," he commented.

"Yeah, he isn't even wearing a diaper," chimed Vanessa.

"I wish I were married and had an egg-baby," said Margo.

"Me, too," said Vanessa. She looked hopefully at Byron.

Byron sighed. "Okay. I'll be your husband," he said. "But only for tonight."

"Who will be my husband?" asked Margo.

"Not me," said Adam defiantly. "I am never, *ever* getting married."

"Jordan?" said Margo.

"Oh, all right."

Surprisingly, Nicky agreed to be Claire's husband.

"Okay, let's adopt babies!" cried Vanessa.

"Adopt them from where?" asked Mal, even though she thought she knew what the answer would be.

"From the refrigerator, of course." Vanessa removed a partially empty carton of eggs from the bottom shelf of the fridge. She set it on the table and opened the lid carefully. "Aw, aren't they sweet?" she said.

"It's the egg nursery," added Nicky.

"Hey, there are enough here for each couple to adopt *two* children," Byron pointed out. "And Mom will still have one left over for tomorrow. Mal, can we? Adopt the eggs, I mean?"

"I suppose so," Mallory replied.

A bunch of hands reached for the carton. They were stopped in midair by Jordan. "Wait! Where are you going to put them? We better fix up rooms or something for them."

"*My* children are not going to live in any Kleenex box," said Margo. "*My* children are going to live in a house. Come on, Jordan." Margo took two eggs and led her brother to the rec room, where she succeeded in talking him into fixing up the dollhouse for their children.

Meanwhile, Vanessa and Byron arranged their eggs in a shopping bag, and Claire and Nicky put theirs in eggcups.

"That's what eggcups are *for*," said Claire.

"Plus, now they're dressed," added Nicky. (Each eggcup was in the shape of a pair of crossed legs wearing blue pants. On the feet were polka-dotted socks and big red clown shoes.)

"We better dress *our* babies," said Vanessa. "I don't want them to go around naked, like Skip."

"How are we going to dress them?" asked

Byron. "I'm not sewing anything. I'll be these eggs' father, but not their tailor."

"Oh, we don't have time to sew clothes," Vanessa replied. "We'll just color their outfits on with crayons." She retrieved a box of crayons from a shelf in the rec room. "Here we go." Vanessa aimed a yellow crayon at one egg. "A nice bright shirt for you. . . . Hey, this hardly shows up at all." Vanessa pressed down harder.

The egg broke.

"Oh! Oh, no! I've killed him!" shrieked Vanessa. "I've killed little — I've killed poor little, um, little — "

"We didn't even name him," said Byron sadly. "Poor egg."

"Poor, poor nameless killed egg," added Vanessa. She was holding the yellow crayon in one hand and the broken egg in the other. The yoke was sliming through her fingers and dripping onto the floor.

Dawn and Mallory both rushed forward — not to comfort Vanessa, but to cup their hands under the egg goo in an attempt to catch it.

"You stay here," Mal said to Dawn. "I'll go for the paper towels."

"The paper towels?!" wailed Vanessa. "Is that all you care about? The rug? Our egg has just been in a terrible accident. If *I* were in a terrible accident, would you run around trying to clean up my blood, or would you — "

"Vanessa! For heaven's sake, it's an *egg*," Mal reminded her.

"And you've only *known* the egg for a couple of minutes," said Dawn.

"I had grown attached," Vanessa replied stiffly.

Mal didn't answer. She ran off, then returned with a roll of paper towels and a plastic garbage bag (degradable). While she and Dawn cleaned up the accident, Vanessa watched sadly. She looked around the rec room at Margo and Jordan, who were putting their eggs to bed in the dollhouse, and at Nicky and Claire, who had loaded their eggs (in the cups) into a doll's stroller and were taking them on a walk to the garage door. Then she looked at Byron, who was lowering their remaining son into the paper bag.

"Mallory, may we please have that last egg?" she asked in a small voice.

"What — the one in the refrigerator?"

"Yes."

"Then we won't have *any* eggs." (Mallory had a sneaking suspicion that a few more accidents might occur.)

"But . . . but . . ." Vanessa's lower lip trembled. "My *baby!*"

"Maybe you should let her have it," Dawn whispered to Mal.

Mal sighed. "Okay. I don't think one egg is worth all this trouble." She turned to her sister. "Vanessa, you can have the egg."

"Oh, thank you! We'll be really careful this time, won't we, Byron? We won't try to dress either egg. They can be naked."

"Hey, you guys!" called Nicky. "We're taking our eggs out to dinner at a restaurant. Want to come with us?"

"Sure," agreed the other kids. And before long, the Pikes had returned to the kitchen and arranged the eggs around the table.

Nicky stood to the side, a dish towel over one arm. "Here are the specials *du jour*," he announced. "Eggs over easy, eggs Benedict, egg salad — "

"Nicky!" cried Claire and Margo.

Mal and Dawn began to laugh. The Pike kids could make anything fun.

CHAPTER 12

"I want a divorce."

"Excuse me?" said Mrs. Boyden.

"I want to divorce Miles."

It was Shawna Riverson who was speaking, and she wasn't kidding. Our Modern Living class had just gotten under way, and I had a feeling it wasn't going to be a typical class. What was typical about a class in which the students got married and had to care for egg-babies?

When we had settled ourselves at our desks that morning, Mrs. Boyden had moved in front of her desk. Usually she sits behind it in a teacher-y sort of way. But on that day, she was wearing jeans and a casual top, and she perched herself *on* her desk.

"Okay, kids, let's talk," she had said. "Tell me how you're doing as couples. Tell me how each of you is doing as half of a couple."

That was when Shawna had said she wanted a divorce.

"Shawna? What's going on?" asked Mrs. Boyden.

"It's just not working out, that's all," she said.

A couple of kids snickered. Shawna sounded as if she were speaking lines from a soap opera. Logan and I looked at each other. *We* weren't snickering. We hadn't laughed much since the night at the movie theater. If something was wrong between Shawna and Miles, I could understand that. Things happened.

Mrs. Boyden didn't laugh, of course. She gazed solemnly at Shawna. "Tell me what's happening," she said.

"I have to take complete charge of the e — of our baby." (Apparently, Shawna and Miles had not named their child.) "Miles hardly ever takes care of it. I lug it around school. I do everything."

Mrs. Boyden didn't so much as glance at Miles. She never turned her attention away from Shawna. "Have you asked him to help?" she wanted to know. "Or do you just expect him to?"

"She just expects me to!" Miles burst out. "She never talks to me. She acts like I'm a mind reader. Like I'm supposed to know everything she thinks or everything she wants."

"Hold on, Miles," Mrs. Boyden interrupted. "Let Shawna finish speaking. Then you can have a turn. Shawna?"

"Well, I shouldn't have to *ask* him to do everything."

"Has he ever taken care of a baby before?" asked Mrs. Boyden.

"I don't know."

"No, I haven't!" exclaimed Miles.

"But the point is, I have this egg all the time," said Shawna. Yesterday I missed half my gym class moving the — the baby around, trying to keep it out of the sun. And I was late to school this morning because I left the egg at home and had to go back for it."

"I see," said Mrs. Boyden. "Miles?"

While Miles spoke, I thought. Shawna and Miles had not named their egg. They didn't want to be bothered with it. As far as Shawna was concerned, having a baby was a pain in the neck. Yet Shawna did treat the egg as her baby. If she'd been totally disinterested, she could have left her baby at home that morning when she realized what she'd done. But she went back for it. I was amazed by how real our children had become to us. On some level, my classmates and I felt as if we were actually married and as if we were actually parents.

Mrs. Boyden was pretty clever. Maybe she was somewhat offbeat, but she was becoming one of my favorite teachers.

"I don't really have time for the egg or for this experiment," Miles was saying, "but I wouldn't, you know, abandon a kid. I'd take care of the egg, if Shawna would ever give it to me."

"Why haven't you ever asked for it?" exploded Shawna. Her eyes had filled with tears. By then, the room was absolutely silent. No one was snickering. No one was even smiling.

Miles looked at his hands, which were folded on his desk. His mumbled answer to Shawna was, "I don't know."

Shawna didn't reply. She turned her head in disgust.

That was when Logan poked me. I leaned toward him, thinking he was going to whisper something about Shawna. Instead, he pointed across the room to two kids I didn't know very well, Angela and Kevin. They were holding hands and Angela was crying. In the emptiness that seemed to follow Miles's statement, Angela raised her hand (the one that wasn't clinging to Kevin).

"Yes, Angela?" said Mrs. Boyden. She handed Angela a box of Kleenex but didn't tell her to stop crying or anything.

I was completely unprepared for what Angela said. I'd thought she was crying because of what went on between Shawna and Miles. Like maybe they reminded her of her own parents. But when Angela said, "Um, Kevin and I lost our baby," I nearly died.

"What do you mean?" asked Mrs. Boyden.

"We lost her."

"We lost the *egg*," Kevin spoke up. "It happened yesterday afternoon. We were at the park. Cathy was with us. She's our egg. I mean, she was our egg. And she was in the box we always kept her in."

"The yellow cookie tin," Angela added.

"Right," said Kevin. "Cathy was with us when we left school, and she was with us when we reached the park. We checked. But when we were leaving the park, we checked again, and the box was empty."

"We tried to retrace our steps," said Angela. "We walked around everywhere. But we couldn't find her."

"We don't know how she got out of the box."

"I feel terrible," said Angela. "Honestly. I mean, if she were really our kid . . . How could we have been so irresponsible?" Angela was crying again.

The room was silent. I suppose everyone was thinking similar thoughts. That in the blink of an eye, anything can happen to a child. You turn around and she's gone — lost or maybe even kidnapped. Or she's eaten something poisonous. Or she's fallen, or been struck by a car. Those things happen every day to all kinds of families.

Angela and Kevin were the first kids in our Modern Living class to lose their baby, and it wasn't funny.

"Are you worried about the grade you'll receive on your project now?" asked Mrs. Boyden, which seemed a little insensitive.

"No!" cried Angela. (She shouted it, actually.)

At the same time, Kevin said, "Yeah, I guess."

Angela gave him a hard look, then softened. "All right, I guess I am a little worried, but that was not the first thing I thought about when I looked in the box and discovered it empty."

Mrs. Boyden nodded. "I understand. Listen, don't worry about your grade. You still owe me a paper, and you can complete it despite what has happened, but some aspects of your project will now change. See me after class, okay?"

"Okay," answered Kevin and Angela.

Mrs. Boyden turned her attention to the rest of the class. "What else?" she asked. She propped her feet on an empty chair. "Anyone?

No one? . . . So things are just fine for the rest of you?"

At that point, I nearly raised my hand. No, things were not just fine between Logan and me. We had nearly lost our own child. We had discovered we didn't quite trust one another as parents.

"Mrs. Boyden?" said a quiet voice.

I turned around. The voice belonged to a guy who was new at school. He'd been paired up with this girl named Zoe.

"Yes, Tarik?" said Mrs. Boyden.

Tarik couldn't look at our teacher. He couldn't look at Zoe or anyone else, either. He stared straight ahead and spoke sort of to the blackboard. "Maybe I should talk to you about this after class, but I — I can't complete the project. I've never had to say that to a teacher before, but it's the truth. I can't do this."

"Why not?" asked Mrs. Boyden gently.

"It's just . . . too much. I mean, Zoe — she's doing her part. But, see, I play two sports and I'm in the choir and I have an after-school job, and my parents are getting divorced and my mom needs a lot of help and I can't do this egg thing, too."

"You mean, caring for a child is more than you can handle at this point in your life? You're overwhelmed?"

"Well, yeah."

"That's okay. Put that in your paper. There is no expected outcome for this project, nothing right or wrong that can be said in your papers. But I'd like to talk to you after class, too. Zoe as well. We'll work something out. Okay. Anyone else?"

Whew. What a class. When it ended, Logan and I just sat in our chairs. Logan doodled. I looked at Sammie, safe in her basket on Logan's desk, protected by more padding than ever.

"I guess that we aren't the only ones having problems," I said.

"I guess not," replied Logan. "In fact, I think we're doing pretty well."

"I bet most parents argue about how to raise their kids."

"Not to mention other things. Like money. My parents had a big loud talk about money last night. That's what they call arguments — loud talks. And they had the loud talk at about two A.M."

"Scary," I commented.

"Yeah." Logan got to his feet. He picked up Sammie's basket.

"I thought you had baseball practice for gym today," I said.

"I do."

"So let me take Sammie."

"Well — "

"You still don't trust me, do you? Just because I lost her for five seconds. Logan, accidents happen. Look at Kevin and Angela."

"I know." Logan didn't let go of Sammie, though.

My eyes filled with tears. "I'll see you later," I whispered, and ran out of the room without Sammie.

"Mary Anne!" called Logan.

I didn't answer.

Logan and I had a long way to go before we reconciled our differences.

CHAPTER 13

Not many days after that memorable Modern Living class, I found myself baby-sitting for Ricky and Rose again. For some reason, I wasn't looking forward to the job. I wasn't dreading it; I just wasn't approaching it with great glee. I wasn't jumping up and down, singing, "Oh, boy, babies! I get to take care of babies again!"

Luckily, Sammie did not come along on the job with me. Logan had taken her home with him.

"This will make the afternoon much easier," I said to Kristy, as we left school that day. "Just *two* babies."

"Yeah. Piece of cake. Sitting for the Rodowsky boys could be much harder. The Walking Disaster and his two brothers. Think what could happen at the Rodowskys' in an afternoon."

I rolled my eyes. "Mayhem," I said. "Chaos. Anarchy."

Kristy smiled. "Oh, there's my bus!" she cried. "I have to go. Have fun this afternoon, Mary Anne."

"Thanks!" I said. "I'll talk to you tonight."

I walked to the Salems' house, dawdling a little. The weather was absolutely gorgeous, warmer than usual, with a wonderful smell of damp earth and new leaves in the air. Perfect baby-walking weather.

I rang the Salems' bell and was greeted by Mrs. Salem, who looked sort of worn out. Her eyes were red, and she seemed saggy.

"Hi, Mary Anne," she said. "Whew. I'm exhausted. The last thing I want to do is go to this meeting, but I'm on the board of the Small Animal Rescue League, so I have to attend."

I hesitated. I wanted to ask Mrs. Salem if everything was okay, but I wasn't sure I should. I mean, adults always ask kids that question, but should a kid ask an adult? I didn't want Mrs. Salem to think I was being nosy. However, *she* had said she was exhausted, so I went ahead and asked.

"Oh, I'm fine," Mrs. Salem replied. "Just tired. The babies seem to be changing their schedule. I never know what to expect. They were sleeping through the night just fine, and now, well, they're not. And they didn't go down for their naps this afternoon until later than usual. So they should sleep longer. You'll probably have a chance to get some homework done this afternoon."

"Great. I was going to take Rose and Ricky for a walk, but I *do* have a lot of work."

Mrs. Salem wrote down the number of the Small Animal Rescue League and reminded me where the emergency numbers were located. Then she left. I watched her back her car down the drive. She was yawning.

I settled myself at the kitchen table with a glass of juice and a bran muffin. I opened the book of short stories we were reading for English class.

" 'The Telltale Heart,' by Edgar Allan Poe," I murmured.

The story was scary. I don't know why I was surprised. Poe's stories are all scary. I was reading along, and my heart was beginning to pound, when something squeaked.

I yelped and knocked over the glass of juice.

"Darn it!" I cried, as juice spread across the Salems' table and dripped down one of the legs and onto the floor.

I mopped it up with paper towels and forgot about the squeak until . . .

"WAHH!!"

I jumped, jerking my hands up and tossing

the book across the kitchen to a counter, where it landed on this bowl of fruit.

"WAHH!" I heard again. It was Ricky. I could tell his cry from Rose's. I could also tell that his cry was going to become a scream.

I ran upstairs and into the twins' room. Ricky was sitting in his crib. His face was red and tearstained.

"Hey, Ricky. What's the matter?" I said soothingly as I lifted him into my arms. "Your mom said you just went to sleep. Why are you up so soon? Are you wet? Or hungry?"

Ricky's answer was a shriek, so I hurried him out of the room before he could wake his sister.

I carried Ricky to the kitchen.

I felt his diaper. Dry.

I offered him a bottle. He fussed and turned his head away.

"What is it? What can I do for you?" I asked.

Ricky drooled and cried.

From upstairs, I thought I heard a whimper, although it was hard to hear over the noise Ricky was making.

"Come on," I said to him. "We'd better check on Rose."

I carried Ricky back upstairs. With every step, his wails seemed to grow louder. "Shh, shh," I said soothingly. "Quiet down."

But he didn't. By the time we had reached

the bedroom, he was throwing his head back and screaming so hard I thought he would choke.

Rose stirred in her crib. Her eyelids fluttered. She was waking up.

I fled downstairs. "Ricky, Rose needs her sleep. Can't you quiet down?" I said. I walked him around the first floor of the house, making a circle from the kitchen to the dining room to the living room, through the hall, and back into the kitchen. As long as I kept moving, Ricky confined his crying to loud whimpers. If I slowed down, the screaming started. I knew what he needed. He needed a walk in the stroller. I was pretty sure that (and only that) would calm him down. But what about Rose? I couldn't wake her up just because her brother needed a walk. I also couldn't check on her while her brother was crying. If I brought him with me, he'd disturb her. If I left him strapped into his high chair or his infant seat, he would begin the awful ear-shattering, choking screaming.

I was desperate.

I phoned my sister.

"Dawn, can you come over to the Salems' right away?" I asked shakily.

"Sure. What's wrong?"

I explained as quickly as I could. "So the thing is," I finished up, "I can't be in two places at the same time. Someone has to take Ricky outside. I've never heard such screaming. Or seen such drooling."

"I bet he's teething," said Dawn. "Give him one of those hard crackers. I'll be over as soon as I can."

"Thank you. You saved my life," I said seriously.

Fifteen minutes later, Dawn arrived at the Salems', sweaty from having ridden her bicycle in such a hurry. I was still walking Ricky in circles around the first floor. He was gumming madly on a teething biscuit I'd found in the kitchen cupboard. The biscuit had quieted him slightly — as long as we kept moving.

"Do you mind taking Ricky?" I asked Dawn. I circled from the dining room into the living room, Dawn at my heels. "I'd take him, but I think I better stay here in case Mrs. Salem comes home. It would probably be better if she found the same baby-sitter who was here when she left the house."

"I don't mind taking him," Dawn replied. "It's so nice out. Where's the stroller? We'll leave right away."

"It's in the garage. Can you wheel it to the front door? I don't want to stop moving until I can put Ricky right in the stroller."

Dawn retrieved the stroller while I circled with Ricky. As soon as she was waiting outside, I made one last circle, but when I reached the hallway, I turned right instead of left, walked through the front door, which Dawn was holding open, and plopped Ricky in the stroller. Dawn was pushing him down the walk before he knew what was happening. Right away, his cries began to fade.

I went back inside and checked on Rose, who was (miraculously) still sleeping. Then I collapsed in an armchair in the living room.

I was just reclining there, enjoying the peace when . . .

"WAHH!"

Oh, no. Not again.

I ran upstairs.

Now Rose was awake, sitting in her crib, screaming and drooling.

"I guess you're teething, too," I said wearily, understanding why Mrs. Salem looked so haggard. "At least I know what to do now. You need a biscuit and a walk."

I found a teething biscuit for Rose — and then realized that in order to take her for a walk, I needed the stroller, of course. I ran to the front stoop and looked up and down the street. Dawn and Ricky had already disappeared. Double darn. So I picked up Crying Baby Number Two and began making the circle. Kitchen to dining room to living room to hall and back to kitchen.

I was still walking Rose when Dawn returned, and Dawn and I were still walking both babies when Mrs. Salem returned.

"Do I *have* to write about that job in the notebook?" I asked Dawn that evening. "I would really rather forget the entire incident."

CHAPTER 14

Ordinarily, when the phone rings at our house, everyone runs for it as if we were going to win a prize for being the one to answer. On the evening after my latest disaster with Ricky and Rose, the phone rang, and *no one* dove for it.

We were all tired.

I was tired from my taxing afternoon. Dawn was tired for the same reason. And Dad and Sharon were tired because they each had had a difficult day at work. Every member of my family was sacked out in a different room.

Ring . . . ring . . . ring.

The phone rang three times before I realized what was happening.

"Dawn, can you get that?" I called from my bedroom.

"Why?" she called from *her* bedroom.

"Because it's *ring*ing."

"Mom'll get it."

"No she won't!" Sharon yelled from down-stairs. "She's too tired."

Ring . . . ring.

"Will someone please answer the phone?" said Dad.

"Mary Anne will!" shouted Dawn.

"I will not! I can't move!"

The phone stopped ringing.

"Did someone answer that?" called Sharon.

"No!" replied Dad and Dawn and I.

"You know, that could have been an important call," said Dawn. "Maybe someone died and left us an island or something."

"A tropical island?" I asked.

"Yes, with palm trees and beautiful sea-shells."

The phone rang again.

I sprinted into Dad and Sharon's room. So did Dawn. We grabbed the receiver at the same time. "Hello?" we said.

"Hello?" said Dad and Sharon on the other extension.

"Hello?" said a fifth voice.

"Logan?" I asked.

"Mary Anne?"

"Okay, everyone can get off the phone," I said. "We haven't inherited an island. This is just Logan calling."

"*Just* Logan?" he repeated. "Thanks a lot."

"Don't be insulted," I told him, giggling, as

the rest of my family went back to being tired. "It's just that — Oh, never mind. It's a long story."

"Oh. Well, I was calling because . . . You won't believe this, but good news! Sammie is walking, and I captured the event on videotape."

I began to laugh again. "A Kodak moment?" I suggested.

"Definitely." Logan was laughing, too.

I knew he was calling so we could talk things out, so we could make up once and for all. "How is Sammie really?" I asked.

"She's fine. How were the twins this afternoon?"

"A mess. They're teething. I'm glad you were taking care of Sammie today. I could *never* have handled her *and* the twins. As it was, Dawn had to come over and help me."

"Wow. I hardly ever hear you say you can't handle a sitting job."

"Sitting is different when babies are involved."

"Yeah. Mary Anne? I'm sorry we've been arguing."

"Me, too," I answered. "It's Sammie and Modern Living. That's why we're arguing. Mrs. Boyden is asking us to do something really difficult — be adults, be married, have babies, and at the same time be kids in school.

I'm glad she didn't give us *real* babies. Can you imagine what shape we'd be in now?"

"For one thing, we'd be broke. Dad took Hunter to the pediatrician for a checkup the other day, and you know what that visit cost? Seventy-five dollars! Seventy-five dollars when nothing was wrong with him in the first place. And we still haven't gotten the bill from the lab for the tests they're doing. Who knows how much that will be for. I don't know how my parents can afford to raise three children. Kerry and Hunter and I are ex*pen*sive!"

"Well, we already know we can't afford even an egg right now, but I didn't expect us to argue so much. I thought that when two people got married they just moved into a nice little place and began hanging curtains and planting flower gardens."

"You mean they played house?"

"I guess so. I never thought about stuff like what to do if you can't find a baby-sitter. Or if you and your husband couldn't agree on how to raise a baby."

"Maybe when you're older you can figure those things out more easily."

"Maybe. I don't think that being older solves everything, though. Look at Dawn's mother and father. Or Kristy's mother and father. Or Stacey's mother and father."

"Yeah. But I bet you have a better *chance* at

a relationship if you wait awhile. Until after college or something.''

''Probably.''

''I mean, we couldn't get married now,'' said Logan.

''We? You and *I*? Get married *now*?'' I squeaked. ''I'll say we couldn't. I want to enjoy the rest of eighth grade first. I want to enjoy being thirteen and not have to worry about all those things I'll have plenty of time to worry about when I'm twenty-two or something.''

''Yeah. I would like to play baseball without first having to think of who's going to watch Sammie. That would be a luxury. I'm not ready for so many complications.''

''Me, neither. Logan, I really like you. I hope you know that.''

''I do.''

''But I'm not ready to be your wife, or anyone else's wife.''

''That's cool. I'm not ready to be a husband.''

''Do you think this is the kind of material Mrs. Boyden wants us to include in our report? What we learned about ourselves?''

''Probably. I think she wants us to consider ourselves as couples and also as the single parts of couples. Remember the questions she asked at the beginning of class one day? The day Shawna said she wanted to divorce Miles?"

"Yeah. Plus we learned some things about loyalty and trust and independence and responsibility. Maybe we should divide our paper into two sections. In one, we'll describe what we learned about ourselves. In the other, we'll describe what we learned about relationships; about the aspects of relationships."

"That's a great idea," agreed Logan. He sighed.

"What's wrong?" I asked.

"Nothing. I'm just sitting here looking at Sammie. When this project is over, I'll kind of miss her."

"Me, too."

"But not *too* much."

"No, not *too* much." I paused. "I wonder what Mrs. Boyden will do with our babies when we don't need them anymore."

"I don't even want to think about it."

"Neither do I. I guess I should go now, Logan. I haven't started my homework yet. But I'll see you and Sammie in school tomorrow."

"Okay. 'Bye, Mary Anne. Love you."

"Love you, too."

We hung up. I headed to my room but detoured down the hall to Dawn's room instead.

I entered it and sat in her armchair.

"What did Logan want?" asked Dawn. She was seated at her desk, writing up a lab report for science class, but she stopped and looked at me. She stuck her pencil in the pencil jar.

"To talk about Sammie. Nothing special, though. You know what I've been thinking, Dawn?"

"What?"

"About the Kumbel catalog. You can throw it away."

"I can? How come?"

"Well, what's *your* opinion about my dad and your mom having a baby now? I mean, what's your opinion since you spent the afternoon with a fussing, teething baby?"

"Oh." Dawn looked sheepish.

"Because *I* was thinking," I went on, "that maybe it isn't a very good idea after all. Not that *we* couldn't take care of a baby just fine. We *are* professional baby-sitters. But a new baby might be rough on our parents at their age. Not that they're old — "

"Of course not," interrupted Dawn. "But they might not be strong enough to go through teething."

"Or to toilet train a kid."

"Plus, they need their sleep now. How could they get up every three hours during the night to feed a newborn?"

"They couldn't. And in about ten years the kid would want to go to Disney World. Do you think Dad would ride Space Mountain with our brother or sister?"

"No way. Mom probably wouldn't, either."

"And you and I would be out of college and living on our own by then," I pointed out. "So we wouldn't be any help."

"That's right."

"Where *is* the Kumbel catalog?" I asked.

Dawn found it in her closet. We opened it to the baby pages we had marked, and we gazed at the pictures.

"Not having a baby will save a lot of money, too," I said, looking at the prices. Baby equipment was not cheap.

"But that little lamp *is* awfully cute," said Dawn wistfully.

"Well, save your pennies," I said. "Maybe one day you can buy it for your own room." Dawn closed the catalog. I stood up. "I'm still curious to know what our baby brother or sister would have looked like."

"And I think it would have been neat if our parents had had a baby of their own. A little Schafer-Spier."

"But I guess it wasn't meant to be."

"I guess not."

CHAPTER 15

It was the last session of our Modern Living class. The following week we would begin a new course — Health. No one was very interested in it, but we had to take it, so complaining was no good. (Miles tried to look on the bright side. "Isn't sex education part of Health?" I heard him say. Logan laughed. I blushed.)

Logan and I walked into Mrs. Boyden's class together. I was carrying Sammie in her basket. Logan was holding our precious term paper. It was 32 pages long, typed, single-spaced. Well, actually, word-processed, not typed. Logan had printed it out on his home computer.

We took our seats, and I set Sammie on my desk. Logan and I watched the room fill up with our classmates and their eggs. Mrs. Boyden was at her desk, thumbing through her lesson book. When the bell rang, she closed the book and stood up.

"Well," she began, smiling, "you've made it. You survived."

"*We* didn't," said Angela. "Kevin and I lost Cathy. We — "

"I meant you survived as married couples," Mrs. Boyden replied gently. "And I'm proud of all of you. Some very heavy issues have been discussed in this class, along with some very personal feelings. Your honesty is what made the class a success. Also, your ability to suspend disbelief. If you hadn't been able to pretend your eggs were babies, you wouldn't have learned so much.

"Today," Mrs. Boyden went on, "I would like each husband and wife to pair up and write a short composition, which will be handed in with your final papers. The subject of the composition is saying good-bye to your children. The time is now twenty-one years in the future. Your babies have grown up, become adults, and finished their schooling. They are ready to leave you and lead lives of their own."

"Logan," I whispered, feeling tearful, "Sammie doesn't need us anymore. She's going to leave us!"

"At the end of the class," said Mrs. Boyden,

"you will leave your eggs behind. They will no longer be your responsibility."

"What are you going to do with them?" asked Shawna.

"Do you really want to know?"

Shawna shook her head. "I don't think so."

"Okay. Break into your pairs, then."

I slid my desk over to Logan's desk, bringing Sammie with me.

"So?" said Logan. "Where's Sammie going?"

"Off to her first important job," I answered. "In New York." (New York is where I hope to land *my* first important job.)

"We're going to let our baby move to big, dangerous New York City?"

"Dear, she's not a baby anymore," I reminded my husband. "She's an adult. She's twenty-one. And she's been offered a position in a publishing house. She will be an editorial assistant. We can't hold her back."

"You're right," agreed Logan.

We wrote our composition and added it to our paper.

After we had handed in our work, I looked at Sammie and said, "I guess this is good-bye. You've been a real — "

"A real good egg?" Logan interrupted.

I made a face at him. But I didn't say anything. I knew he was joking around because he didn't want to get sentimental in class, where everyone could see him. Some men have such a hard time dealing with their emotions.

That afternoon our BSC meeting was attended by seven humans and no eggs. Although earlier I had been sad about letting Sammie go off to New York, I was now feeling quite free. I wasn't the only one.

Stacey bounced into club headquarters crying, "Freedom at last!" She sounded the way most kids do on the day summer vacation starts. "No more mixing bowl," she went on, "but I *do* miss Bobby . . . sort of. Well, just a teensy bit."

At 5:28, Jessie ran into the room, the last club member to arrive. As she settled onto the floor next to Mallory, she looked around, then asked, "Where are your babies?"

"Gone," said Kristy sadly.

"They grew up," added Dawn.

"Mine went to New York to start a career," I said.

Jessie and Mal did not know *what* we were talking about, so we described our last Modern Living class to them.

"Cool. What are the rest of your children doing?" asked Mallory.

"Bobby is going to teach high school history," said Stacey.

"Izzy became a car mechanic," said Kristy. "He opened a garage in Stamford. I made him promise to visit every Sunday."

"My baby is going to become a famous artist," said Claud. "Naturally."

"Mine's in medical school," said Dawn.

The phone rang then, and we arranged a job for Claudia with the Newtons.

"You know what I think?" I spoke up after a break in the conversation. "I suppose if I absolutely *had* to, I could raise a child of my own. But I wouldn't want to. I'm too young."

"Also, your dad isn't ready to be a grandfather," said Stacey.

"No, I'm serious, Stace. I'm not kidding around. Do you think you could be a parent right now? I mean, if you'd just given birth?"

Stacey frowned. "No. I really don't. How would I support a baby? Anyway, I don't *want* to be a parent. Not yet."

"You're right," I agreed. "I could only raise a baby if I lived at home and Dawn and Dad and Sharon helped me. I couldn't do it by myself."

"I do want to have kids someday, though," said Dawn.

"Definitely!" agreed the rest of us.

"But maybe when I'm older," she went on.

"When I'm twenty-five. Maybe even thirty. You know, now lots of women are having their first baby when they're *forty*. Or older. I'm not in any hurry."

"Me, neither," I said, "but I don't want to wait until I'm forty. Twenty-five sounds like a good age."

"I'm going to have eight children, like my mom did," commented Mal.

"It's a good thing you won't have them all at once," replied Stacey. "You might want to quit after one or two."

"Maybe. Anyway, I don't have to decide now."

"And in two years you'll take Modern Living," said Kristy, "and you can do a trial run with just one egg-baby."

"I hope my first baby is a girl," said Jessi dreamily. "I will name her Mary Rose. I've always wanted a daughter named Mary Rose."

The phone rang again then, and our meeting became busy with BSC stuff. No one mentioned the eggs again.

When Dawn and I reached home that evening, we received a call from Sharon, saying she and Dad would be about half an hour late and asking us to start dinner. So we did. As we took things out of the fridge and set them on the kitchen table, Dawn said, "Mary Anne, do you think you'll ever be able to eat eggs again?"

I shook my head. "Not for a long, *long* time."

"I know what you mean."

My sister and I began chopping vegetables for a salad. "I sure am glad," I said, slicing a carrot, "that we didn't say anything more to our parents about having a baby."

"Whew, I'll say," agreed Dawn.

"Can you imagine if we had convinced them and your mom had gotten pregnant right away and then we had finished Modern Living and had changed our minds?"

"We would have been a little late."

"Yeah, just a little."

"Is being a little late like being a little pregnant?" Dawn asked.

I laughed. "I guess so. Either you are or you aren't."

Dad and Sharon entered the kitchen just in time to hear that last part of our conversation.

"Who's having a baby?" asked Dad suspiciously.

"No one, thank goodness," I answered. "No one we know of."

"How's dinner coming, girls?" asked Sharon.

"It's ready," I said.

"Let's eat," said Dawn.

"Let's eat in the dining room," added Sharon.

"Ooh, special occasion?" I asked.

Sharon shrugged. "Maybe, maybe not."

We sat at the dining room table and passed around the salad and this Chinese vegetable dish Sharon makes and brown bread and these vegetable patties that are supposed to look like hamburgers but don't.

When our plates were full, Sharon looked at Dawn, then at me, and smiled. "Girls," she said, "Richard and I have been thinking about your wish for a baby. You haven't mentioned it for awhile, but we know that doesn't mean you aren't still *think*ing about it."

I know my face turned pale then. I felt faint. Across the table from me, Dawn's eyes widened to the size of basketballs, and her hands began to shake. Oh, *no*. Why couldn't parents just forget things once in awhile? Why did they have to remember everything?

"Um," I said.

"Um," said Dawn.

"See, the thing is, Dawn and I talked about it and we realized we shouldn't have . . ." My voice trailed off.

"Don't worry," said Sharon. "It's okay. Richard and I have discussed everything and we decided if you really want something to care for, you may get another pet. Tigger might like some company."

I let out the breath I was holding. Oh, a *pet*. I managed a grin at Dawn, who grinned back. "Do you want a pet?" I asked her.

"Do you?" Dawn countered.

"Not really. Tigger's enough."

"That's how I feel. . . . But thanks, Mom. Thanks, Richard."

"Yeah, thanks," I said.

Dad looked surprised. "We thought you'd jump at the chance to get another pet."

"We might have, if it weren't for Modern Living," I replied.

"Modern Living?"

"Yeah. Dad," I said, "you have no idea how hard it is to be a parent."

Dear Reader,

In *Mary Anne + 2 Many Babies*, the members of the Baby-sitters Club take care of many infants. If you are going to baby-sit for an infant, it is important to be prepared. Baby-sitting for an infant is very different from sitting for an older child. You might think it will be easy because you don't have to entertain an infant. Wrong! If you're going to sit for an infant, there's a lot you need to know. Babies can't tell you what they need, so you have to be prepared. In fact, don't be surprised if parents with a new baby don't call you right away with a sitting job. There's a good chance they may ask a sitter who's older, or even an adult. A good way to show clients that you are capable of taking care of a new baby is to take an infant care course. Check with the Red Cross or the Y in your community to see if they offer such a course. When I was thirteen, I took a course at my church. Another way to learn how to take care of a baby is to start out as a parent's helper — helping out while the mom or dad is at home. Believe me, they'll welcome the help!

Happy reading,

Ann M. Martin

L. GODWIN

Ann M. Martin

About the Author

ANN MATTHEWS MARTIN was born on August 12, 1955. She grew up in Princeton, NJ, with her parents and her younger sister, Jane.

Although Ann used to be a teacher and then an editor of children's books, she's now a full-time writer. She gets the ideas for her books from many different places. Some are based on personal experiences. Others are based on childhood memories and feelings. Many are written about contemporary problems or events.

All of Ann's characters, even the members of the Baby-sitters Club, are made up. (So is Stoneybrook.) But many of her characters are based on real people. Sometimes Ann names her characters after people she knows, other times she chooses names she likes.

In addition to the Baby-sitters Club books, Ann Martin has written many other books for children. Her favorite is *Ten Kids, No Pets* because she loves big families and she loves animals. Her favorite Baby-sitters Club book is *Kristy's Big Day*. (By the way, Kristy is her favorite baby-sitter!)

Ann M. Martin now lives in New York with her cats, Gussie and Woody. Her hobbies are reading, sewing, and needlework — especially making clothes for children.

Notebook Pages

This Baby-sitters Club book belongs to _____ .

I am _____ years old and in the _____

grade.

The name of my school is _____ .

I got this BSC book from _____ .

I started reading it on _____ and

finished reading it on _____ .

The place where I read most of this book is _____ .

My favorite part was when _____ .

If I could change anything in the story, it might be the part when

_____ .

My favorite character in the Baby-sitters Club is _____ .

The BSC member I am most like is _____

because _____ .

If I could write a Baby-sitters Club book it would be about ___

_____ .

#52 Mary Anne + 2 Many Babies

For a short time, Mary Anne and Dawn think it would be a great idea to have a new baby brother or sister. This is what I think of the idea: _____

_____. If I could have any number of brothers and sisters, I would want _____ brothers and _____ sisters. I would want _____ older brothers and _____ older sisters, and _____ younger brothers and _____ younger sisters. If I could choose to be the oldest one or the youngest one in my family (or one in the middle!), I would want to be _____ _____ because _____

_____

_____. If I had to take care of a baby brother or sister, these are some things I would be sure to do: _____

_____

_____ .

MARY ANNE'S

Party girl -- age 4

Sitting for the Pikes is always an adventure.

Sitting for Andrea and Jenny Prezzioso -- a quiet moment.

SCRAPBOOK

*Logan and me.
Summer luv at Sea City.*

Illustrations by Angelo Tillery

*My family...
Jeff, Dad and Sharon,
Dawn and me. And Tigger.*

Read all the books
about **Mary Anne**
in the Baby-sitters Club series
by Ann M. Martin

Mysteries:

Portrait Collection:

100 (and more)
Reasons to Stay Friends Forever!

More titles... ▶

❑ MG48225-4	#81	Kristy and Mr. Mom	$3.50
❑ MG48226-2	#82	Jessi and the Troublemaker	$3.99
❑ MG48235-1	#83	Stacey vs. the BSC	$3.50
❑ MG48228-9	#84	Dawn and the School Spirit War	$3.50
❑ MG48236-X	#85	Claudi Kishi, Live from WSTO	$3.50
❑ MG48227-0	#86	Mary Anne and Camp BSC	$3.50
❑ MG48237-8	#87	Stacey and the Bad Girls	$3.50
❑ MG22872-2	#88	Farewell, Dawn	$3.50
❑ MG22873-0	#89	Kristy and the Dirty Diapers	$3.50
❑ MG22874-9	#90	Welcome to the BSC, Abby	$3.50
❑ MG22875-1	#91	Claudia and the First Thanksgiving	$3.50
❑ MG22876-5	#92	Mallory's Christmas Wish	$3.50
❑ MG22877-3	#93	Mary Anne and the Memory Garden	$3.99
❑ MG22878-1	#94	Stacey McGill, Super Sitter	$3.99
❑ MG22879-X	#95	Kristy + Bart = ?	$3.99
❑ MG22880-3	#96	Abby's Lucky Thirteen	$3.99
❑ MG22881-1	#97	Claudia and the World's Cutest Baby	$3.99
❑ MG22882-X	#98	Dawn and Too Many Baby-sitters	$3.99
❑ MG69205-4	#99	Stacey's Broken Heart	$3.99
❑ MG69206-2	#100	Kristy's Worst Idea	$3.99
❑ MG45575-3		Logan's Story Special Edition Readers' Request	$3.25
❑ MG47118-X		Logan Bruno, Boy Baby-sitter	
		Special Edition Readers' Request	$3.50
❑ MG47756-0		Shannon's Story Special Edition	$3.50
❑ MG47686-6		The Baby-sitters Club Guide to Baby-sitting	$3.25
❑ MG47314-X		The Baby-sitters Club Trivia and Puzzle Fun Book	$2.50
❑ MG48400-1		BSC Portrait Collection: Claudia's Book	$3.50
❑ MG22864-1		BSC Portrait Collection: Dawn's Book	$3.50
❑ MG69181-3		BSC Portrait Collection: Kristy's Book	$3.99
❑ MG22865-X		BSC Portrait Collection: Mary Anne's Book	$3.99
❑ MG48399-4		BSC Portrait Collection: Stacey's Book	$3.50
❑ MG92713-2		The Complete Guide to the Baby-sitters Club	$4.95
❑ MG47151-1		The Baby-sitters Club Chain Letter	$14.95
❑ MG48295-5		The Baby-sitters Club Secret Santa	$14.95
❑ MG45074-3		The Baby-sitters Club Notebook	$2.50
❑ MG44783-1		The Baby-sitters Club Postcard Book	$4.95

Available wherever you buy books...or use this order form.
Scholastic Inc., P.O. Box 7502, 2931 E. McCarty Street, Jefferson City, MO 65102

Please send me the books I have checked above. I am enclosing $_____
(please add $2.00 to cover shipping and handling). Send check or money order—
no cash or C.O.D.s please.

Name_____ Birthdate_____

Address _____

City_____ State/Zip _____

BSC596

THE BABY-SITTERS CLUB®

by Ann M. Martin

Meet the best friends you'll ever have!

Have you heard? The BSC has a new look — and more great stuff than ever before. An all-new scrapbook for each book's narrator! A letter from Ann M. Martin! Fill-in pages to personalize your copy! Order today!

☐ BBD22473-5	#1	Kristy's Great Idea	$3.50
☐ BBD22763-7	#2	Claudia and the Phantom Phone Calls	$3.99
☐ BBD25158-9	#3	The Truth About Stacey	$3.99
☐ BBD25159-7	#4	Mary Anne Saves the Day	$3.50
☐ BBD25160-0	#5	Dawn and the Impossible Three	$3.50
☐ BBD25161-9	#6	Kristy's Big Day	$3.50
☐ BBD25162-7	#7	Claudia and Mean Janine	$3.50
☐ BBD25163-5	#8	Boy Crazy Stacey	$3.50
☐ BBD25164-3	#9	The Ghost at Dawn's House	$3.99
☐ BBD25165-1	#10	Logan Likes Mary Anne!	$3.99
☐ BBD25166-X	#11	Kristy and the Snobs	$3.99
☐ BBD25167-8	#12	Claudia and the New Girl	$3.99
☐ BBD25168-6	#13	Good-bye Stacey, Good-bye	$3.99
☐ BBD25169-4	#14	Hello, Mallory	$3.99
☐ BBD25169-4	#15	Little Miss Stoneybrook...and Dawn	$3.99
☐ BBD60410-4	#16	Jessi's Secret Language	$3.99
☐ BBD60428-7	#17	Mary Anne's Bad Luck Mystery	$3.99

Available wherever you buy books, or use this order form.

Send orders to Scholastic Inc., P.O. Box 7500, 2931 East McCarty Street, Jefferson City, MO 65102.

Please send me the books I have checked above. I am enclosing $_____ (please add $2.00 to cover shipping and handling). Send check or money order—no cash or C.O.D.s please.

Please allow four to six weeks for delivery. Offer good in the U.S.A. only. Sorry, mail orders are not available to residents in Canada. Prices subject to change.

Name_____ Birthdate ___/___/___
    First   Last   D / M / Y

Address_____

City_____ State_____ Zip_____

Telephone (____)_____ ☐ Boy ☐ Girl

Where did you buy this book? Bookstore ☐   Book Fair ☐   Book Club ☐   Other ☐

■ SCHOLASTIC

BSCE396

THE BABY-SITTERS CLUB®

by Ann M. Martin

Collect and read these exciting BSC Super Specials, Mysteries, and Super Mysteries along with your favorite Baby-sitters Club books!

BSC Super Specials

More titles ➡

The Baby-sitters Club books continued...

Now THE **BABY·SITTERS CLUB**®

★ is a Video Club too! ★